The
Merlin
Prophecy

*"A mystic legend and his crusade
into the new world"*

Jeff Berg

iUniverse LLC
Bloomington

THE MERLIN PROPHECY
"A MYSTIC LEGEND AND HIS CRUSADE INTO THE NEW WORLD"

This is a work of fiction. All of the characters, names, incidents, organizations, and dialogue in this novel are either the products of the author's imagination or are used fictitiously.

iUniverse books may be ordered through booksellers or by contacting:

iUniverse LLC
1663 Liberty Drive
Bloomington, IN 47403
www.iuniverse.com
1-800-Authors (1-800-288-4677)

Because of the dynamic nature of the Internet, any web addresses or links contained in this book may have changed since publication and may no longer be valid. The views expressed in this work are solely those of the author and do not necessarily reflect the views of the publisher, and the publisher hereby disclaims any responsibility for them.

Any people depicted in stock imagery provided by Thinkstock are models, and such images are being used for illustrative purposes only.
Certain stock imagery © Thinkstock.

ISBN: 978-1-4917-1314-3 (sc)
ISBN: 978-1-4917-1316-7 (hc)
ISBN: 978-1-4917-1315-0 (e)

Library of Congress Control Number: 2013919686

Printed in the United States of America.

iUniverse rev. date: 11/7/2013

To my family who have always been there for me
on a variety of levels, bless you all

The soul of man is immortal and imperishable.
—Plato

Prologue

It has been suggested that before the big bang and birth of our known universe, there was only the vast void of cold, dark space. Winds of gases created a multitude of gigantic, swirling tornadoes everywhere. Each one produced points of friction that spontaneously igniting specks of matter into existence. Over time, these tiny pieces of pure energy grew independently and exponentially into immensely expandable cocoons, filling themselves with all the required universal components. Ultimately bursting into enormous, blinding, silent flashes, ejecting precious life-giving elements into each universe.

An oval-shaped celestial rock moves quickly across the great expanse. A closer inspection reveals a spongelike, porous surface with a frosty, hollow core and a curious block of an icy bluish substance lying dormant. The shape gives the distinct impression of some sort of egg, naturally designed and released from beyond our known mapped universe, no doubt created for some specific reason. Perhaps its purpose is to ignite something into existence or even enhance established life. It passes several spectacular wonders occurring in an endless cosmic dance with enormous multicolored gas nebulas, planets, asteroids, and exploding stars. It passes by our nearest neighboring galaxy, Andromeda; sails across the event horizon of an enormous black hole; and enters our Milky Way Galaxy. It finds its way to our solar system and gets pulled into the asteroid belt's gravitational field for a while. Suddenly, an asteroid bumps it, sending it on a direct collision course with a huge monolithic body of rock, deflecting it out toward Earth.

Chapter 1

After the fall of the mighty Roman Empire, hell on earth was unleashed, ushering in the darkest of days. Europe was constantly bombarded with ominous, life-changing events, from the black plague to romantic tales of chivalrous knights and ruthless kings waging wars for supremacy. Surreal moments of sheer madness ran wild throughout the roads of every city, town, and village.

There have been a variety of conflicting stories involving a man known simply as Merlin. Most believe that he came from the minds of imaginative storytellers, whereas a few firmly believe that he was once very much human. Truth be known, he was considerably much more than human and became a legend because of it. His mother was Princess Alden, who always maintained she had never been alone with another man for any reason. Because of this, rumors circulated that Merlin was the spawn of Satan, an incubus, or perhaps even a product of immaculate conception. He became many things to many people, comfortably wearing a variety of hats throughout his life. Among his many talents, he was a musician, bard, kings counsel, alchemist, prophet, and master magician, and according to local lore, he was referred to as a demigod. In South Wales, United Kingdom, in AD 679, constant battles shook the lands over Europe's blood-drenched fields, providing an endless supply of death, despair, and disease. People could find moments of peace only in one of three places: on a mountain, deep inside a rainforest, or in death.

Alden was the youngest, smartest, and bravest of the three daughters of the tyrannical Welsh king of Dementia. She was shocked and frightened at becoming a pregnant virgin and did her best to hide the pregnancy from everyone, especially her father. She knew the king would surely have her exiled or killed in disgrace, but Alden desperately wanted her unborn child to live. She made arrangements for sanctuary with the head priest of the St. Peter's church in Carmarthen, South Wales, where she vowed to serve God and raise her child in peace. One night into her sixth month, she went to the stables, stepped up into her small horse-drawn carriage, and grabbed the reins with a distinct expression of determination on her tear-bathed face. She took a deep breath and began moving past the blood-stained castle walls, out into the cold darkness of uncertainty. Now safely at the church, with the sisters' help, Alden soon began to relax, and gave birth to an unusually hairy, albeit healthy, male child. She named him Merlinus. His initial physical appearance managed to frighten the nuns. Even the head priest, Father Angus, clutched his crucifix and knelt down to pray, baptizing him on the spot. At the age of five, a healthy and happy lad, Merlinus soon became affectionately known as Merlin by the sisters. He again startled everyone when he suddenly began speaking in completely lucid, intelligent sentences. He practically lived in the church library, reading on a variety of subjects, like a human sponge absorbing all he could. At the age of ten, with the help of his teachers, Merlin learned to read and speak Welsh, French, English, and Latin. He was also a typically curious lad who got into his share of trouble, but he always knew that true power is knowledge. He quickly became the precious jewel of St. Peter's church, loved by all. Father Angus did what he could to help guide Merlin into manhood. At fifteen, he became a strapping young lad with a wealth of education and everything in front of him; his mother could not have been prouder. Merlin's grandfather, the king, eventually received word that his daughter and her child were alive and living in a church in South Wales. He instantly dispatched a band of assassins to kill everyone in the church, including the royal embarrassment and her bastard child. The next night, the king's men lit the church ablaze killing anyone who tried to escape. Merlin's mother screamed as fire begins to engulf her room. She tells her son that her father's assassin knights were there to kill them both. "You must leave right now, and don't look back! My journey is over, but yours has yet to begin. You were meant to live a long life and accomplish many great things." She told her son to stay in the shadows and seek shelter deep inside the nearby rainforest. She handed him a blanket and told him to stay safe and warm. Merlin hugged his mother for the last time. The fire quickly intensified as he went to the window, jumped out onto a nearby branch, climbed down the tree, and darted out into the dense black forest, completely undetected. His mother watched him disappear and then bravely died quietly.

On his horse, the assassin leader yelled out, "What of the woman and child?"

Seconds later, another voice responded, "Adults only, my lord; the child is nowhere to be found." The king's men ventured into the forest as far as their horses would allow. "If the boy is alive, he would not last two days in there."

Not long after, they exited the forest as quickly and silently as they had come. Merlin found cover behind some rocks, where he lay down, quietly curled up, and emptied all the tears he had bravely suppressed for hours, releasing them with all his heart and soul. After a while, the initial grieving process began to subside as he collapsed from exhaustion. Hours later, just before dawn, young Merlinus opened his eyes and got up to take one last look at the only home he'd ever known, which was now smoldering ashes. Haunted by the faint screams of the dead blowing through the dense trees, he took a long, deep breath. He then brushed himself off and headed into the heart of the forest, seeking shelter to honor his mother's last wish—his survival. Distraught and lost, Merlin became painfully aware that he might have to live in that inhospitable forest for the rest of his life. Fortunately, he had learned a variety of survival skills from the head priest, who was the closest thing to a biological father he had ever known. Trudging deeper into the forest until he could walk no more, he closed his eyes and fell down onto a soft, marshy area. The next morning broke to reveal a lightly frosted ground as a teary Merlin shivered uncontrollably, wrapped in the blanket his mother had given him. Praying to God for the sun's merciful warmth as his eyes began to well up, again missing his saintly mother, he got to his feet and soldiered on. Several hours later, he collapsed again by the foot of a large hill. He clearly heard the sudden sound of rushing water and looked around, desperately struggling to locate the source of the sound. The mountain mist slowly burned away, revealing a lush multicolored oasis brimming with life. Warming rays of sunlight caressed a calm wall of sparkling water that fell gently into an emerald-colored pool. Merlin could not believe his eyes and quickly began to drink the cool, fresh water, submerging himself fully and gaining strength with every gulp he took. Still standing in the waterfall, feeling rejuvenated, he opened his eyes and focused on what appeared to be the mouth of a large cave. He slowly walked toward it, and his eyes got wide with disbelief as he found himself inside a large crystal-lined cavern. After a quick reality check, he went back outside and, with a renewed sense of purpose, noticed a school of fish in the pond and discovered edible berries on a bush nearby and had his fill. Recalling his survival lessons, he made a stone fire pit inside the cave and started a fire. After warming up, he began to make himself at home as he fashioned a spear for a fish dinner. After his first good night's sleep in days, he decided to create a large work table and other forms of home comfort using various forest materials. Much to his surprise, he quickly grew accustomed to forest dwelling, finding his rhythm and soon feeling human again. Merlin soon discovered that one of his favorite things was performing magic tricks. He imagined that he was a world-renowned traveling magician with a sack full of spellbinding tricks that would always leave his audience in awe and begging for more. He worked hard, honing his survival skills and dreaming of becoming the greatest wizard the United Kingdom had ever known. Merlin had always loved heights, so it seemed natural for him to climb the inviting front face of his new humble abode. He soon found a stone shelf high above the cave's entrance, overlooking the entire tree line of the rainforest. There he would dream of future days and gaze, mystified, at the star-filled night sky.

Chapter 2

One clear evening, on his new sky-view ledge, as always, he looked up into the heavens. Out of nowhere came a deafening silence that surrounded Merlin with a sense of fear. He could not even hear the chirp of a cricket; it was as if time itself had simply stopped. He then heard a low hum and turned to see where the sound might be coming from. He looked to his left, and his jaw dropped when he spotted something on fire in the sky, seemingly headed toward him. He attempted to convince himself that the object was most likely a flaming projectile from a nearby rogue catapult at the edge of the forest. As it got much closer, Merlin stood up and breathed easier, knowing that it would most certainly pass right over him. As it did, its reflection blazed in Merlin's eyes as he tracked it across the sky. As the flaming foreign object sailed just overhead, its heat warmed Merlin's body and took the chill out of the cool night air for a couple of seconds. He instantly realized that the angle was too high to have tossed by any catapult, deducing that it must have come from a higher source. He watched in amazement as the fallen star easily blew through treetops like a tossed pebble through a spiderweb. The sound of the impact was a muffled thud when the object landed in a nearby soft hillside, close enough for him to see its final stop. *A star of my very own!* he thought with excitement as he laughed with delight for the first time in a long while. Anxious as Merlin was to see it up close, it was too far away for night travel. He would try to sleep and would have to wait until daylight before setting out on the reasonably short but arduous journey through the forest. Early the next morning, the elated, starstruck lad grabbed a few provisions and rushed out to see his celestial rock up close. He finally reached the impact site in the hillside as the scene began to slowly reveal itself through the morning mist. The sun rose higher, revealing a smoldering hole at the soft base of a hillside near the edge of the forbidden forests. He slowly peered inside to see an oval-shaped, porous rock with a faint bluish glow emanating from within its core. The odd light quickly faded as the tiny star became cool to the touch. The porous, coral-like rock was surprisingly light, so he decided to make a netting with some rope he'd fashioned from vines and carefully carry this otherworldly object on his back to his humble abode for a closer examination. After finally reaching the cave, excited and exhausted, young Merlin gently placed the foreign object on the table. He then lit a fire and took a seat in amazement on a chair in front of it. Using two long, narrow crystals, he carefully began to chip away pieces of its shell to expose its core.

He removed a large section of the star, exposing a gelatinous blue substance. Cautiously, he poked the thick, globular fluid with one of the crystals, just as it almost appears to move on its own. Soon the Jell-O-like substance thinned out, seemingly reacting to the warmth from the proximity of the fire. Not noticing the dramatic change in the core, the young lad tossed another log on the fire and paused to watch the flames' light refracting off the cave celling as the now-lively alien liquid moved quickly up the narrow crystal. Without a hint of warning, the liquid engulfed his hand and moved up his arm, quickly covering his entire body with a blue hue, causing Merlin to go into shock and drop to the ground, losing consciousness. He woke the next morning groggy, confused, and completely unaware of what had happened, but overall, he felt surprisingly good. He walked outside and stood under the cold water, where he soon became aware of the amount of strength surging through his body, the alertness in his brain, and his heightened senses. Feeling a bit overwhelmed, he automatically thanked God and prayed for guidance; as he breathed deeply, he was humbled in this most unprecedented moment. He started to become acutely aware of what was taking place in his body. While processing the implications of these gifts, Merlin stumbled on a loose rock and fell backward onto a sharp edged crystal that left a two-inch gash in his upper left thigh area. Merlin's natural impulse was to scream in agony; instead, he looked down at the wound and watched in bewilderment as the hole quickly and painlessly closed. His immune system and overall brain functions had been strengthened, pushed beyond basic human limitations. The surreal transition of having full access to brain functionality and possible extreme life longevity took a bit of time to adjust to. For good measure, young Merlin stepped back directly under the refreshingly cool waterfall. He took a couple of long, deep breaths, closed his eyes, and slapped himself twice, once on each cheek. He slowly opened his eyes, realizing without a doubt that this experience was quite real. Merlin had to remain grounded and come to terms with being more than merely human. He had to adjust quickly and cultivate these gifts to help others. He felt very much alive and fearless with his newfound alien abilities. To his amazement, he later discovered that he could float weightlessly upon a thin cushion of air whenever he felt at peace, usually during his meditation sessions. Next, he found that he could move things with his mind. Many years later he would also sadly discovered that he was unable to produce offspring of his own.

One early morning, Merlin woke up frightened in a cold sweat, realizing that he could experience future events that seemed more real than being awake. He knew he must learn to hide his newfound abilities or be branded an outcast, a demon, or perhaps the devil himself. On a midsummer day, while hunting with spear in hand and tracking wild boar, he chanced upon a small, well-hidden druid village. He instantly recalled a story his mother had once told him of a mystical druid priest she knew and how they could be trusted and even admired as honorable aboriginal monks of the British Isles. They were known for their ability to jump from the human world into another realm—the otherworld. Stories of a magical doorway into a parallel universe intrigued Merlin immensely. He humbly introduced himself and soon after they adopted him and he became known as Saltus Puer, the forest child, finally finding the family he so desperately needed. After a soothing hour of floating meditation in his private oasis, Merlin gazed at his reflection in the pond and thought, *What a blessing it is that I have the look of my mother, having never met my father, if there ever was one.* Thanks to his teachings, Merlin had always kept an open mind and suspected that the earth was completely round just like every other viewable large body in the sky, not flat with an edge that led down to hell, as some believed. Merlin believed that fear was the biggest disabler among most people who completely believed that escape meant certain death. Merlin would slip away for extended periods of time back to his lair of solitude. He had to continue honing his alien abilities and conduct all of his private works. Every now and then, he ventured outside the great forest to the nearest town for supplies. Years later, he began recording his life's work in the form of memoirs, prophecies, and magical secrets all in one large leather-bound book. A few centuries later, an extremely healthy middle-aged looking Merlin ended up working closely with three kings in a variety of capacities, such as prophet, astronomer, bard, military adviser, and counselor, and he finally achieved his lifelong dream of becoming the supreme magical entertainer loved by all, especially children everywhere.

All he ever really wanted was to help ease people's pain. He had always loved working with his hands and soon became a master alchemist and sculptor in his spare time. Merlin's visions were realistic nightmares that tormented his soul from time to time. Periodically, he witnessed monumental events that always seemed to end in total annihilation. Merlin quickly learned that the scariest thing about these nightmares was the inability to close his eyes or turn away from the horror. But these were the Dark Ages, and anyone alive then felt the ominous evil that loomed. Time passed on a gracefully aging Merlin as future visions continued to appear in his sleep. One particular vision of events concerned and intrigued Merlin more than most. In the first vision, he saw two suspicious and powerful men in formal new-world attire. These men were unquestionably planning what seemed to be the end of the world. A series of large black *x*'s marked the dates on a nearby calendar over most of the summer of 2013. Almost seamlessly, another scene emerged as a man-made sign standing in front of a large building that clearly read The Roslin Institute of Technology. He then saw a man in uniform reading some loosely folded black-and-white printed pages—a copy of the *Edinburgh Newspaper*, dated in the year 2013. The next images were of the inside of the structure, which was a sparse and sterile environment with shiny, smooth tabletops and strangely shaped, mechanical objects on top of them. A small group of oddly dressed people with masks were performing some sort of highly advanced medical procedure over their patient's body. Controlled lighting emanating everywhere within the ceiling and walls fascinated Merlin. He was startled when he noticed that the patient was an exact mirror image of himself as a much younger man; he instantly thought that a dream had entered his vision state and was playing with his mind. He stared at the face closely, when the patient's eyes opened suddenly, shocking Merlin out of his vision and into a cold sweat. He ran outside to revive himself in the waterfall. He had a revelation and somehow instinctively realized what it all meant and what he must do. Excited over the implications, he began to prepare for his rebirth in the new world. Every once in a great while, a unique individual got the chance to rise above the mundane from a common, two-dimensional, lost-in-the-crowd existence—Merlin was such a man.

Chapter 3

Madness ran up and down the cobblestone road in every town of every country across Europe as battles raged constantly. Innocent people were enslaved or butchered, leaving bloody trails for the Black Death to follow, as if the perfect storm over Europe had granted Satan his personal playground. Peace was rare and could generally only be found in between battles, after the final plunge of a sword. Many years later, the gracefully aged Merlin, now looking to be somewhere in his eighties, completed his life's works in a large book—one of his finest accomplishments— stamped with his personal seal of a large *M*. He then drained an ounce of his high-octane blood into a small, thin vial and placed it inside the spine of his book. Merlin was not the first magician of his kind, but with his close royal connections, sharp mind, and cosmic talents, he became the greatest there ever was or would be. Now, as he neared the twilight of his extremely long life, his dream visions became increasingly intense. He saw great upheaval all over the world as modern wars and mass human exterminations were executed without remorse or concern of consequence. The one common thread in these dream visions was that they all directly or indirectly involved Merlin, and he wondered how this was even possible. He concluded that no matter what, he must remain strong and free until his last breath. Merlin then decided to create a large golden statue of a dragon to be used as a diversion and a bargaining chip for his future attempt into the new world, as he had envisioned. He then decided to create a treasure map and hide it in the lining of the book. He spent several months in his cave, perfecting a finely crafted solid-gold dragon statue with brilliantly laid diamond clusters on its teeth, talons, and tail, and two large red rubies for its eyes. It was AD 1094. Merlin had always enjoyed putting on magic shows, especially for the children, with grand performances using fireworks at night in the main square in every town or castle he frequented. One of Merlin's last official performances was in Scotland. It was filled with hope, merriment, and wonder—while the devil patiently waited outside.

One fine, warm day, Merlin was about to deliver another inspiring performance for the children when a tower scout rang the warning bell, looked down and yelled, "We have company, my lord—a small group of men on horseback!"

Without pause, Merlin replied, "Very well then—open the gate, lad!" With archers poised and trained on the uninvited guests, the visitors slowly approached the castle's main gate.

The lead knight clearly announced, "We are the appointed protectors of the church known as the Knights Templar, and we are here to speak with a man who calls himself Merlin."

Wearing his signature theatrical black cloak for the show, Merlin walked through the main gate, instantly recognized the banner of the Knights Templar, and ordered the bowmen to stand down as he stretched his arms wide and said, "Welcome, my knightly Roman brothers. How may I serve you on this fine day?"

The lead knight slowly dismounted and, trying desperately not to stare at the strangely dressed old man before him, carefully asked, "Excuse me, sir—are you the magician known as Merlin?"

With a big grin, Merlin responded, "You have found the man you seek." The young knight handed Merlin an officially sealed scroll, written by the hand of His Holiness the pope. Appearing a bit speechless, Merlin broke the seal and quietly read the letter.

Greetings, Master Merlin,

I am a great admirer of magical acts, and tales of your performances are of legendary proportion. I therefore hereby cordially invite you to my home at the Vatican to meet with me to entertain about fifty humble servants of God, including myself, along with a few hundred orphaned children. You will, of course, be compensated generously and have the church's everlasting gratitude. If you accept, my most trusted young knights will accompany you safely to Rome and back.

The letter was signed by Pope Urban II. Without skipping a beat, Merlin said, "I am committed to a performance tonight and will not under any circumstance disappoint the children. Please stay for the night as my guests and enjoy the show! I will arrange for your horses to be tended to, and we can leave in the morning."

Weary from their journey, the knights happily agreed, much to the delight of a rejuvenated Merlin. Before the main event, he sat and feasted with the good knights. He overheard one of the knights talk of a small, private library vault filled with books, documents, and priceless treasures inside the main building of the

Vatican. Merlin had always had a passion for book collections, rare as they were, and he couldn't think of a safer place for his book to be kept until his hopeful return into the new world.

The next morning, Merlin set off for Rome to meet the pontiff. After a long, arduous journey, an elated pope welcomed him at the Vatican. Introductions were formally exchanged. Merlin was given the royal treatment, which included food, drink, and regal accommodations provided by the gracious host. The next day, fully rested, Merlin and the pope became more personally acquainted, chatting for several hours in the main courtyard, much to the pope's delight. Hundreds of wide-eyed, orphaned children leading a much larger crowd of people headed directly to the main stage by the courtyard. The pope said, "For the next couple of hours, you, my magical friend, will be the center of attention, and for that, I am eternally grateful. I look forward to your performance and dinner afterward."

Merlin humbly bowed. "As do I, Your Excellency."

Merlin put on the most amazing show ever witnessed by an audience anywhere, including a spectacular fireworks display that lasted over an hour. Merlin was then invited to meet with His Eminence privately that evening for some tea and a chat. They feasted like kings. His Holiness stared intensely at Merlin, as if in deep thought, and then politely asked if he would consider coming back again for another performance.

"It would be my honor, Your Holiness. It was a great deal of fun for me as well."

Following a fine dining experience, the pope invited Merlin to his private office for a drink to cap off what ended up being one of the most memorable events ever. Humbled and thankful,

Merlin knelt down and kissed the pope's ring. "Name your fee, anything you wish—anything at all."

Merlin paused for a couple of seconds and replied, "My lord, I have worked extensively with some very generous kings, yet none of them were able to help me with one simple need that I believe only you can provide."

"Then it is to be my honor to grant the great Merlin the Magnificent his only wish. Name it, my son, and it's yours, with all my heart."

Merlin softly chuckled and said, "I am in dire need of a place in which to keep my book safe and unmolested through to the next millennium, and what safer place in the world could there possibly be?"

The surprised pope immediately scratched his head and said, "This is all you desire—for us to safeguard a book?"

Merlin smiled and nodded. "Yes, my lord, that is all I require." He reached deep into his cloak and produced a large metallic box with a magical flair only Merlin could achieve.

The puzzled pope agreed to Merlin's odd request. "There must be something else I can do for you—this hardly seems an even trade."

"Okay then, how about world peace?" Merlin jokingly replied.

An unexpected tear dropped from the pope's cheek, and he said, "That is all I want as well. I am determined to think of something else more appropriate I can do for you. We are the only recognized religious center on this continent in these ungodly times, a standing testament to God's plan. We are never really, truly alone as we navigate through this surreal time together, for God is with us always."

"I have encased my book in lead to preserve it from the elements for all time."

With another curious expression, the pope asked, "Curious—what use is an unreadable book?"

"That brings me to the second part of my request, and it's going to seem even stranger still."

Now at the edge of his seat, the pope said, "Please, do continue."

"I humbly request that you write an official letter to the future pope of the year 2013—I will dictate what to say. It is imperative that this stays a secret; the fate of the future may depend on it."

The humble pope agreed as he eagerly wrapped the lead box inside a thick regal-blue velvet cloth. Merlin then said, "This must remain untouched for a millennium, at which time a priest chosen by the new world pontiff of 2013 will remove it and follow your handwritten letter of unusual instructions."

The pope agreed to his fascinating new friend's request, odd as it was. He completed the letter, and they walked together to his modest but safe library. "I plan to construct a fortress for my books and bobbles one day." Merlin watched with the curiosity of a child as His Holiness lit a wall torch and opened the thick metal door. He then gently placed the lead-sealed book inside a small compartment in a corner of the room.

On their way out, the pope said, "You have so impressed me that I am going to do two things that I have never done before—two things that have never been heard of, for that matter. First, I am going to give you six of my strongest and bravest young knights to protect you with their lives for as long as you walk this earth. I have already sent word to them; they will be assembled and ready to meet you in the morning. Second, my door will always be open to you and your men for as long as you wish."

Completely humbled, Merlin's eyes welled up with tears, and he knelt down again, swaying his head from side to side in disbelief. "Kings have never been so kind. I do not have the words to thank you enough, my lord."

The embodiment of Christ let out a rumbling laugh. "Merlin, my friend, you yourself might just well be the greatest gift of all; it is I who should thank you." The highly amused pope smiled and nodded as if he had found the Holy Grail itself. "So you see, I am being selfish and merely protecting my investment." He gently hugged the overwhelmed wizard. Pope Urban took a deep breath and added, "I have a very important speech to make at the council in Clermont and must take my leave early in the morrow."

The next day, a well-rested Merlin quickly sprung out of bed and excitedly went to meet his private band of knights.

He went outside toward the front gate, where the knights waited quietly for their new assignment. They happened to be the same familiar six young knights who had escorted Merlin to Rome. The men already admired and respected their new master, making it easy for him to execute his plan to create a business partnership for their future. "Good morning. I am Merlin, and I do hope that you enjoyed last night's performance!" They all smiled and nodded. From left to right, one after another, the six knights proudly introduced themselves. "It is indeed my honor and privilege to know you fine men. We will be staying on here as guests for a short while, as offered by His Holiness. I know that you are all good men—strong, passionate, and true, with more to offer others than the tips of your swords. From this day forward, you men are more than just warrior knights. You are to be trained as stone masons to help rebuild our fallen walls. Across the land, people will know you as the last line of defense, and you will be praised as enforcers. You and your families will be well compensated for your work and dedication."

That afternoon, Merlin hired two master stone builders to train his men how to build various stone structures both large and small. A bit apprehensive but eager to learn, the apprentice knights soon surpassed the masters in their teachings. Merlin then told his knights that they had entered a new world that would always be financially rewarding through hard work and total commitment. Days later, Merlin had a clear vision of his Masonic business surviving well into the new world and becoming one of the elite secret organizations in history. He burned key ideas into his men's minds in a straight and plain fashion. "I am not a leader; I am just an old man with a vision. You are now brothers of a special order, and the keys to the future lie with your male children, their male children, and so on, assuring the knightly bloodline flows for a millennium and beyond. The only way to ensure its success is to keep it a secret society, or it will all be for nothing. A tree is only as strong as its roots—as above, so below." Merlin's physical light was finally extinguished in his sleep while he was surrounded by his third generation of trusted knightly brothers. They placed him in an unmarked stone coffin and sealed it inside his cave, alongside his golden dragon, just as he had requested.

Chapter 4

In the spring of 2013, in the Vatican, the pope sit's alone quietly in his chambers staring at an ancient sealed scroll written by the blessed Pope Urban II himself. Taking great care, he broke the seal and began to read its contents. Eloquently written, it instructed him to find a strong, seasoned, and slightly unorthodox priest for a secret assignment of the highest order. The scroll stated,

> This man is hereby requested to be temporarily excused of his duties for the sake of protecting the integrity of the church and will be allowed to return with a full pardon and support upon completion of the assignment. This mission is to be considered dangerous and quite possibly pivotal to the fate of the world, so you must choose wisely. He is also to be discreetly funded by the church for anything he requires, without pause or question. There is a private letter of instructions waiting for him in a sealed envelope hidden inside a large lead-covered box in the library.

The pope immediately remembered the infamous ancient, mysterious metallic box with *MMXIII*—2013—etched on its surface, wrapped in an old cloth and displayed in a glass case. Feeling humbled, the pope summoned his top advisers immediately for consultation. After hours of deliberation, with the aid of a few bishops, they narrowed the choices down to a few candidates, and then he finally chose the most likely candidate. They unanimously decided on father Frank DeCarlo, an unconventional, healthy middle-aged priest who cares deeply for God and the fate of the world. His extensive work toward world peace made him stand out among hundreds of other candidates.

Currently working in the Philippines, a profoundly surprised Father DeCarlo received an order by the pope himself to return to Vatican City immediately. He got on the next flight to Rome, attempting to ascertain what the emergency could possibly be. Having never met His Holiness, the priest went over in his mind how the meeting might play out. Upon arrival, the pope summoned him to his chambers, where His Holiness got right to the point, explaining the situation and reading the letter as mandated by Saint Urban II. The priest knew that he had to take the assignment all on faith as he accepted this most unusual request by His Holiness. Father DeCarlo knelt down to kiss the pontiff's ring and was promptly blessed. Just then, much to the priest's surprise, he was officially relieved of his duties and Roman collar. Temporarily decommissioned and feeling somewhat confused, Mr. DeCarlo was then handed a no-limit Vatican Bank gold card. "Please take good care of this, my son; I expect it back when this is all over."

"Of course, Your Eminence—is there anything else?"

The pope nodded and put his hand on Frank's shoulder. "God be with you, my son!" The pope called for his personal secretary to escort Frank down to the library and hand him the mysterious lead box from inside a glass case.

"I know the item of which you speak, Your Eminence; it will be done." Still in a bit of a fog while walking down a corridor, Frank saw a wall-hung crucifix, cast his eyes upward, and quietly whispered, "I sure hope you're watching this."

Inside the high-security library vault, the secretary went right to the glass case, extracted the object, and handed it to the now ex-priest. He immediately stuffed it into a large pouch of a leather shoulder bag graciously provided by the secretary. Frank always wore his faith well, and it would no doubt be put to the test soon enough. As the ex-priest exited the Vatican, his thoughts began to run wild, even for him. He stopped before getting into the taxi, took a deep breath, and decided that whatever happened, he would remain grounded, focused, and as prepared as he could. He had to believe that God had chosen him for a reason, but somewhere in a corner of his mind, Frank couldn't help but get the distinct impression that he had just traded his soul for a greater good. Either way, it was a done deal, so he headed out to a nearby hotel, where he could examine the contents in private.

Once he was safely inside the room, Frank immediately locked the door, found a table, and removed the old lead box from the bag. He put it down gently on the table, grabbed a large knife from the kitchenette, and carefully cut a large slit into the soft lead cover. He then picked the book up and shook out an ancient sealed envelope inscribed with the words *Statuto Unum* (*The Appointed One*). He took a deep breath, collected his thoughts, cracked the seal, and began to read.

Dearest Sir,

You have been carefully chosen for your worldly experiences and slightly unorthodox ways, and they will both assuredly be put to the test. You are hereby requested to take a leap of faith and follow these instructions as requested. First, you are to procure a modest countryside inn near a place known as the Roslin Institute, located somewhere in Edinburgh, Scotland. Inside the box is my life's work in book form; it is now in your charge. Hidden inside the spine is a flat glass vial of dried blood. This next part will be a stretch for you to accept, but accept you must. You are to remove the bottle and persuade the leader of this advanced medical facility to apply the sample into producing a human body—mine. My given birth name was Merlinus, but I was more commonly known as Merlin. Among other things, I have been given the gift of seeing future events, and I have had the good fortune of witnessing my own rebirth within this medical structure. God willing, we shall tempt our fates and perhaps do some good in your world if we are successful. This event and my identity are to remain secret, known to you alone. I look forward to meeting you, my first new-world friend-to-be. I am confident that you will succeed. Thank you for your trust and cooperation in advance.

Your hopeful future friend, M.

Having trouble processing the scope of this letter, all Frank could think was *Merlin—the magician?* Giving his head a shake, he looked around the room as if some kind of prank were in play, but there was nothing unusual to be found. He then completely cut off the top of the box and removed an old, large leather-bound book titled *Merlinus Scriptor Libri Prophetiae* (*Merlin's Book of Prophecy*). He found and removed the cleverly hidden vial of blood in its hollow spine and held it up to the light. In awe, he thumbed through the well-preserved pages, each one more remarkable than the next. The dumbfounded ex-priest quickly decided to take advantage of a nearby library and do some research on this assumed mythical mystic. He soon found information in a famous book entitled *The Black Book of Carmarthen* considered to be the oldest known book of the early history of Wales. Skimming through the ancient text on microfiche, he found that this book had several blurbs pertaining to an actual, enigmatic man known simply as Merlin. It was well documented that Merlin had once been an exceptional man of many talents. Frank read on to find out that Merlin had apparently been much more than just a magician. He had been a bard, musician, war strategist, and trusted counsel to kings, but unknown to most, he had also been a prolific prophet.

Back at the hotel, Frank was still skeptical but armed with a bit more knowledge about the man once called Merlin. He placed the book in his leather satchel, headed to the airport, and boarded the next flight to Scotland for a country inn rental, as requested. Two days later, the ex-priest entered his new scenic country inn, courtesy of the church. The appointed one took a few deep breaths, picked up the phone, and called the Roslin Institute, as instructed. He managed to arrange a meeting with the head professor for the following morning.

Early the next day, as the sun gently bathed the frosted hillsides, crystalizing the moment, Frank stepped outside his temporary, rustic abode and prayed for forgiveness for any acts against God he might be compelled to commit. Frank sat down on a bench by the front door while he prayed. He soon composed himself and vowed to remain open-minded and humble under the eyes of God as he followed this most unusual path developing before him. With the purplish vial tucked in his pocket, Frank left for his appointment, silently praying all the way there. Inside the main office of the Roslin Institute, Professor Jack Bristol, a mild, gray-bearded gentleman in a white coat and bifocals, diligently worked away at his computer. The seasoned pioneer and his crack team of fellow scientists had performed cloning experiments on plants and animals and, most recently, had conducted top-secret human stem cell research. Dr. Bristol had recently been considering retiring and conducting lectures at a local university. He had always dared to dream of successfully cloning a human body ever since Dolly had been brought into existence, as human cloning seemed the next logical step.

At the main gate, a security guard gave Frank simple directions. Inside the building, he gingerly knocked in front of an already-wide-open head office door. The professor jetted up from his chair to meet him. "Mr. DeCarlo, is it?"

"Yes, it is, but please call me Frank."

"It's a pleasure to meet you, Frank. Won't you come in? And please excuse the mess! As you could imagine, we don't get many visitors here ever since Dolly." He turned to show Frank his computer desktop photo of the perfectly cloned ewe. "At the time, we thought that her existence had elevated the world of science to the next level. We were inaccurate. My wife said that I loved that sheep more than I loved her." He looked over to the picture again. "I don't know; maybe she was right—at the time." They both shared a brief smile. Then the professor said, "Now, what could I possibly do for you, my good man?"

Armed with only his faith, his wits, and access to unlimited funds, he confidently replied, "I have in my possession a sample of what I believe to be blood, and I need it analyzed." He reached into his jacket pocket and held up the ancient vial.

The professor slowly got closer to the oddly shaped object, took it from Frank, and held it up to the light. He took his time and looked at its contents as he cocked his head to one side and squinted with interest. "Interesting—if I had to guess, judging by its purplish hue, it is most likely old animal blood mixed with blueberry juice." He turned to Frank and smiled. "You can't be serious, but if you are, I think someone may be playing a joke on you, yes? So it's not a complete loss, I'll give you twenty euros for the bottle to add to my collection."

Frank shook his head with a hint of confidence. "I assure you, Professor, this is no joke. I have traveled thousands of miles to reach this point, and I'm a firm believer in destiny. I represent a highly influential group of people who have been known to be most generous to get what they want. I was chosen specifically for this assignment for my tenacity and better-than-average negotiating skills." Frank then thought to himself, *Better-than-average negotiating skills? Hmm, I have persuaded people to come to church—no actual lie there.*

With no facial expression, the professor replied, "Just what exactly are you suggesting that I do?"

"I suggest that if whatever is in this vial proves to be human and usable, my people are willing to have you well compensated for your services for producing a clone."

The professor sternly responded, "Animal, mineral, or vegetable?"

"We believe animal—of the … human persuasion."

"Sir, I have been a scientist for a very long time, and I'm telling you that this is not human. My dear sir, I am truly sorry, but it's simply not possible."

Frank had come prepared. He pulled out a short stack of hard currency to erase any trace of doubt regarding whether or not this was a joke. "This is yours for just analyzing it—no strings attached. I just need the truth, and you seem like an honorable man. If it turns out to be a usable human sample, as we believe, my people are willing to offer you two hundred thousand euros upon completion. I imagine that would go a long way into your pending retirement, would it not?"

The professor accepted the initial offer by quickly taking the cash from Frank's grasp with a smile. "Yes, yes, it would at that. I will require roughly one hour. You can wait here or go down the hall to the cafeteria for breakfast, if you wish."

An hour later, Frank returned and found the professor staring strangely at the oddly hued substance under a scope, in its natural liquid form. He went back and forth on three occasions, looking at the blood-analysis report and back to the scope. Finally, the dumbfounded professor, stumbling over his words, said, "I am humbled in thinking that I have seen it all, but this is truly unusual. The sample appears to contain equal parts of human and an unknown DNA sequencing that our database does not recognize. Normally, my decision would be a decisive and resounding no for several reasons, not to mention the moral and legal ramifications. Having said that, there seems to be an element that could conceivably strengthen every system in its host, acting as a kind of super-blood, if you will. What is encouraging is the fact that this strange hybrid blood may possess the ability to actually heal itself from any infection and literally regenerate new tissue from the cellular level spontaneously.

"I can't believe what I am about to say, but the body that hosted this blood must have been an immortal being of sorts, giving him perfect health and what must have been extreme life longevity. An extensive preliminary test clearly shows that this blood sample is not in our mainframe database, rendering it incontestably … alien. This may be the fountain of youth—the Holy Grail, conceivably worth billions of euros. Where on earth did you get this?"

"That, my dear professor, I'm afraid is confidential."

Dr. Bristol nodded. "Yes, of course, but if we do this, I will require the help of two other trusted scientists, and I must be protected from the media and general public—no one can know." Giddy as a homeless man who had just won a lottery, in his mind, Dr. Bristol began to go over all the necessary equipment required.

Frank smiled and said, "This is our wish as well; the procedure must be kept secret at all cost."

"I just happen to have a fully equipped private facility downstairs that will serve just fine. We even have an amniotic fluid chamber—of my design, I might add. We're going to require twenty-four hours to properly prepare for the procedure. Mr. DeCarlo, I cannot stress this point enough: new management is taking over in six months, and they'll be recruiting the next generation of brilliant young scientists. So unfortunately, my time here is limited, but theoretically, we should have enough time for the patient's body to mature fully if all goes as expected. If the blood works as I believe it will, you should be leaving this facility with a highly genetically enhanced, healthy adult clone." With the deal struck, the professor said, "I can't think of a better way to cap off my career. I will have to arrange for the rest of the staff to be put on temporary leave with pay for six months. I don't expect much resistance, considering how quiet things have been lately."

Frank left and received a call from the professor two days later, as expected.

Chapter 5

"The building has been evacuated, and we are now fully prepped and ready to begin the procedure. You are most welcome to stay as my guest, of course, and observe the entire procedure."

Bursting with anticipation Frank had not experienced since he was a boy, he called a taxi immediately and headed to the institute. Three weeks later, inside the professor's amniotic tank and tethered to an artificial umbilical cord, a tiny new cloned human fetus floated. It soon began growing rapidly, as expected. Two weeks later, they carefully extracted it from the artificial womb, and it soon began breathing oxygen on its own. They watched in utter amazement as newly dubbed subject HC13—human clone 2013—began growing rapidly before their eyes. The professor became concerned when he noticed an unusual amount of hair growth all over the infant's body, but it quickly shed the hair, exposing a perfectly normal, healthy toddler. Video cameras were soon installed in key areas of the locked facility to record the incredible day-to-day metamorphosis. While reviewing a live video feed of the small boy clone in his office, the astonished professor sat back and shook his head in disbelief at Frank. "It would be difficult to convince anyone that these videos are in real time. I don't believe it, and I'm watching it live."

In utter disbelief, all Frank could do in response was shake his head, shrug his shoulders, and instinctively cross his arms over his chest.

They hoped that the antigrowth hormone injections would slow the aging process down. They knew the shots should theoretically be effective, but this was, of course, an unprecedented procedure where almost anything could go wrong. They figured that without the hormone, the subject would quickly age, wither, and die in just under twelve months at the current accelerated growth rate. The professor explained to Frank that he would probably either be escorting an old man or a corpse out of the building in about four months' time. Frank thanked the professor for his candor as they both again stared at the rapidly growing child in awe. "We'll do what we can to prevent that, so hope for the best, but plan for the worst."

As it turned out, the subject's growth rate did miraculously begin to slow down substantially just as he reached his peak—that of a healthy young adult, which was exactly what they had all hoped for but was realistically the last thing they had expected.

A few months later, HC13 lay mute and motionless on the cold steel table. Dr. Bristol privately announced to his colleagues as they stood over their patient, "I can't decide if we should be toasting to the birth of the world's first perfect human clone specimen or sneaking out the back door after creating a modern-day, mindless Frankenstein." After a short session of grappling with his demons, the professor concluded that he had indeed ultimately fulfilled his dream by successfully producing the world's first healthy human clone. HC13 was, however, an emotionless mute—but he was still a fully physically functional, strapping young lad. A modest gym area served to help strengthen the subject's already-well-defined body through long-distance treadmill running, lifting heavy weights with ease, and stretching his body to its limits. The perplexed Dr. Bristol and his colleagues examined the patient's brain extensively using everything available, including spectral analysis. Brain images should have lit up like a pinball machine, showing his brain to be off-the-charts active, but nothing like that occurred. Physically, he's a perfect specimen who also happened to be a dumb mute.

"By all accounts, this alien blood should be giving him full brain capacity to the extent of perhaps even telekinesis, and yet he remains totally unresponsive."

The professor turned to Frank and said, "I find this most unsettling, and I wish that we could study him longer, but we're almost out of time." The professor graciously excused himself and dashed out, grazing a piece of equipment on the way. One of the professor's colleagues turned to Frank. It was hard to tell if Dr. Bristol had just had an epiphany or if he'd suddenly really had to go to the loo. The second doctor snorted with laughter, causing a well-deserved release of emotion from all three men. Minutes later, Dr. Bristol appeared at the doorway, completely out of breath and unable to speak. The three men again laughed.

The professor caught his breath to say. "Do you remember when the great Oz gave the scarecrow a brain? We can do that; we have in our possession an artificial brain." After several minutes of consultation, the three doctors unanimously agreed to cheat life by surgically implanting the patient with an artificial microprocessing unit. The professor explained to Frank, "We have decided to use a cybernetic implant. It will act as a brain within a brain that should help to educate the subject anytime he accesses the one-and-a-half terabyte hard-drive computer—complete with everything we know about the universe and our world to date. This miniature processor carries countless pages of data, images, and videos that should theoretically give him the essentials to survive in this world. The only drawback is that it's the first prototype of its kind and has never before been tested. Partnered with that is an external multifunctional voice-activated Bluetooth device—a jet-black streamlined ear-mountable unit with a mini, retractable high-definition eye screen for private viewing. This highly advanced component will jack directly into a mini-port to be installed just behind the patient's right ear.

"If that's not enough, it also includes a fully preloaded musical library that plays most anything on command. A homing chip will also be implanted in his chest for safety reasons and peace of mind in the event that he somehow gets lost or in case something goes wrong." With the subject well sedated, the professor took a scalpel and made a deep two-inch incision across his right thigh. Seconds later, the incision closed up almost as quickly as it had opened as they stared in near disbelief. The professor also recommended that HC13 be given proper instruction in reading, writing, mathematics, and some basic social skills. The entire procedure took just under eight hours and was declared a complete success after they ran a battery of tests. Dr. Bristol then announced, "He is strong and highly resilient; I have every confidence that he will do what he is here to do—whatever that may be."

Frank looked down at the unconscious clone and smiled. "Yes, of course. I'm sure you're right, Doctor; thank you for everything you've done."

One late night two weeks before the deadline to vacate, the fully formed, empty-minded clone lay in his bed and slowly closed his deep green eyes to sleep. He unconsciously became fixated on the dangling crucifix around the ex-priest's neck. Frank prayed silently with his eyes closed by the patient's bedside, as he had done every night since HC13 had drawn his first breath of air.

HC13 fought to keep his eyes from closing, but his lids finally won the battle, and he was lulled into a dark, silent void. Suddenly, he began to envision frightening bursts of blinding light, but he was unable to wake. Synced with each flash was the pounding of his heartbeat. The flashes sped up as if an old movie projector had automatically powered up on its own. Soon a spectrum of vivid colors as images began to form and slowly come into focus. In his first dream, ancient images of Merlin's past flowed into view, and he vividly saw them one frame at a time. He saw Merlin's birth, his saintly mother, the burning church, his fallen star, his friends and loved ones, the faces of the children he entertained, bloody battles, his book, Pope Urban, his knights, his crystal cave, the shimmering waterfall, and, finally, his death. HC13 woke up, gasping for air from the shock of being jolted into a new reality, which had instantly transformed a mindless clone into Merlin, who quickly began to fully regain consciousness. His eyes darted around feverishly, looking at what appeared to be a dimly lit room, not noticing Frank fast asleep in the darkest corner of the room. Still in a horizontal position, he began moving his hands and feet, making sure that he was all there. A fascinated Merlin accidentally found the light switch and began turning it on and off like a child with a new toy. Frank woke up and slid forward off the chair onto the cold linoleum floor, clutching his crucifix. Their eyes locked, and Merlin's face began to display an expression of relief as a tear of joy trickled down his cheek. Frank watched as his eyes lit up with elation a mindless clone could not possibly display. The highly emotional clone was about to speak, when Frank swiftly got up off his knees, moved closer, and discreetly but firmly whispered, "Don't say a word; do not even look like you have something to say! If you understand me, blink your eyes once!" HC13 responded with one clear blink over a blank expression. "Good—very good." Glancing up at a video camera peering directly down from above the foot of the bed, Frank softly added, "We are being watched carefully by the people responsible for creating your new body." Peering eye to eye, he said, "They're looking for anything unusual." The priest gave his head a shake, and thought to himself, *This is really happening—God help me!* "I am Father Frank DeCarlo, the appointed one and your humble servant, my lord. It is the year 2013, and we are at the Roslin Institute in Edinburgh, Scotland. I believe your recent erratic movements went unnoticed, or someone would be here by now. To ensure your safety, you must not speak and must appear to be completely mindless, void of any thought whatsoever until we are free and clear of this facility. Do you understand?"

Merlin promptly responded with another single clear and resounding blink.

"I will notify our kind hosts that we will be leaving this place later today. The professor and his team are going to perform one last series of tests, as previously agreed." It was a bit earlier than the normal wake-up time, but Frank couldn't wait and notified the professor of his intentions.

The professor complied with Frank's request. "Of course, as you wish, but it will take an hour to prep for the final tests. I took the liberty of procuring some casual street clothes for your new friend." He removed a pair of blue jeans, a white T-shirt, a jean jacket, and sneakers from a clothing store bag.

"That was very considerate of you, Professor—thank you."

The professor thanked and excused his two colleagues and conducted HC13's final tests on his own. After everything checked out perfectly, he spoke to Frank privately. "Your new friend must be given a name along with proper identification, so you may have to perform an illegal act. Forged identification papers must be drawn up for him if he's to live a reasonably normal life—if that's even possible."

Frank responded, "Message received, and I assure you, Professor, that he will get the best care and guidance money can buy. Speaking of money, I took the liberty to prepare this cashier's check for two hundred thousand euros, as agreed. Enjoy your retirement, my friend!"

Dr. Bristol looked directly at HC13. "I think that I will miss you most of all, Scarecrow," he said, patting his crowning achievement on the shoulder. "Remember that he should periodically jack into a computer for software upgrades."

They both wished each other luck as they carefully helped the clone into the backseat of a waiting taxi. Merlin the clone was finally set to begin a new life in a world only he could have dreamed of. With an open window, he breathed in the fresh country air as he attempted to maintain control and simply enjoy the ride.

Chapter

6

They arrived at the inn, and Merlin slowly spoke for the first time. "Thank you for the ride; it was fun."

Frank awkwardly smiled at the driver. "Uh, he's new in town."

The driver replied, "No kidding?"

The reborn demigod immediately began to indulge his senses, filling his lungs with country-fresh new-world air as Frank paid the driver. As they approached the house, Merlin stopped to enjoy the vibrant scene by breathing deeply, savoring the moment. Trying desperately to accept the situation he found himself in, the appointed one said, "This is the inn you requested; I hope it serves, my lord. Your book is safe inside as well."

Beginning to regain confidence in his speech, Merlin responded, "I am no one's lord; please address me as Merlin!" As he saw his reflection for the first time, he moved closer to get a better look at the young, vibrant man he once was. "How many people get a second chance and are aware of it?"

"I imagine that you are the first, Merlin."

Merlin turned toward Frank and gave him a hug. "Thank you for my new life, my friend. All I want to do right now is enjoy several hours of my first real sleep in centuries; I'm sure I'll feel more like myself shortly thereafter."

"Yes, of course. I'll show you to your room." Frank immediately removed a couple of steaks from the freezer to thaw out for dinner. Merlin slept well right through the day and woke up just in time for dinner. Frank awkwardly showed his friend how to use the toilet and shower and then said, "You must be hungry; I'll begin preparing dinner for us. There is a wine cellar in the basement with several dusty bottles—join me?" He went out back and tossed two big, juicy T-bones onto a flaming grill. Once they were both seated with full plates and glasses, Frank thanked God for the meal and prayed for guidance on the path that lay before them.

Wrapped in a new large black robe provided by Frank, Merlin sighed and said, "I absolutely love the toilet and especially the shower. I was not aware of these wonderful advancements." After enjoying a hearty meal, Frank lit the fireplace. As Frank poured the second bottle of wine, Merlin said, "When I was a child, I encountered a fallen star carrying an alien substance that was completely absorbed into my body. It changed everything, giving me the ability to see things far into the future. I can also float weightlessly above the ground on a cushion of air during periodic moments of bliss. I can also move objects through thought."

He gave Frank a small demonstration by lifting the wine bottle up off the table.

"Later, I discovered that I have been blessed with extreme life longevity, baring witness to centuries of bloody barbarism and injustice." Filling his lungs again, he quickly gulped down a full glass of wine.

Frank refilled their glasses again and said, "I am only going to ask this once: Is there any evil at play here?"

With a playful grin, Merlin replied, "Evil is generally always at play, because people will always be willing to be puppets for his amusements." The appointed one listened carefully, respecting Merlin's extensive experiences and accomplishments in awe. Merlin continued, "I must assure you, my new-world friend, that I am the furthest thing away from Satan there is." He paused and then added, "Albeit in the old world, some might have disagreed with that. I am compelled to believe that my being here is through God's good grace, allowing me a second chance to help in any way that I can."

Completely convinced by Merlin's response, Frank pursed his lips, nodded, and had another gulp, which undoubtedly helped him relax more.

Merlin grinned and sighed heavily. "I tried hiding who I was from the very beginning, but after serving and outliving four kings, befriending the pope, and entertaining countless people over the course of four long centuries, it became increasingly arduous to remain an unknown, as I'm sure you could imagine. For that reason, this time, I have the chance to be a commoner and experience this life freely and virtually invisible." He looked outside at the beautiful sunset over a mountain. With a serious expression, Merlin leaned forward, gazing directly at Frank. "All my future-event visions have always involved me directly or indirectly in some form or another. The seeds I planted grew around the world and still thrive today. At the twilight of my extremely old age, six young knights were given to me by the pope to protect and obey me as long as I walked the earth. I began a secret organization known then as the Knights of the Brotherhood of Masonry. Through one of my dream visions, I witnessed its growth well into this century as top Masonic officials

The next morning, Frank prepared breakfast and set out alone for the University of Edinburgh, leaving Merlin alone as he began to meditate. On the university campus, Frank met with several students, none of whom were willing to help. Frank was about to leave, when a young, attractive female student approached him. "Excuse me, sir, but I was just wondering what it is you are attempting to do here?"

Frank explained the situation briefly, to which she replied, "I'm Michelle Dubois, a journalist major from France."

"My friend and I are relatively unfamiliar with computers, and I am prepared to pay generously for your time."

Being a free spirit, Michelle had always been open to new things, so with just a shade of apprehension, she took a moment and then said, "The extra money would come in handy, and you seem trusting almost enough to be a man of God."

Frank replied with a smile, "Very good then; we'll meet tomorrow at the café in the main square for lunch together with your new student."

She firmly replied, "I look forward to it."

Chapter 7

At the head of the United Grand Lodge of England sat the pro grand master, Sir Gabriel Hammond. Well spoken and always impeccably dressed in his imported Italian suites, this six-foot-five 320-pound man always made his presence felt wherever he went. His circle of associates knew him as an intimidating and ruthless tyrant with little patience for incompetence. Those closest to Gabriel described him as a borderline psychopath trimmed with narcissistic tendencies. He was second only to the grand master himself, and if for any reason the GM was unable to attend a function or was gone for any length of time, the pro grand master was to take the lead position. Next on the chain of command was the deputy grand master, Sir Seth Hamilton. A cross between a GQ wannabe and a weasel, a much smaller-framed man was responsible for all formal interactions concerning most regions and relations in the UK. His influence extended beyond the Masonic walls and included high-security access to a covert unit from an independent department of Interpol. If Satan had had sons, Seth would have been one of his favorites. Further down the chain of command was the assistant grand master, Sir Reginald Anderson II, who was currently on a well-deserved two-month trip around the world with his family. Just below him was the honorable grand secretary, Sir Joshua Rigby—a dedicated and humble knight who always seemed to make time to help those in need without breaking his own stride, as all knights should. His job was coordinating and scheduling special events as well as the day-to-day tasks befitting members of the great hall and surrounding members throughout the United Kingdom. Gabriel's father was a high-ranking Masonic official who had married into a prominent family. Since Gabriel was a small boy, he had always believed that his destiny was to be the youngest Masonic grand master in history. Few people ever got their childhood wish granted, but with a strong desire and an influential support system in place, anything was possible.

That night, back at the inn, Merlin dreamed. Flashes of his happy band of ancient knightly brothers appeared, warriors to the end, defending the defenseless, as true knights should. Merlin woke up in a cold sweat, wondering if his mere presence would be enough to stop the madness or if the bell had already tolled. Frank soon arrived with word of his success in procuring a suitable tutor, whom they were to meet later that day. After their traditional morning meal, they went to the town square. Merlin marveled at almost everything he saw; he was like a toddler in a room full of bubbles. Michelle got out of a taxi and approached the busy square. She was dressed in heels, a summer skirt, and a thin white blouse; her long, curly dark hair blew gently in the warm breeze. Heads turned as she made her way toward the café. She soon spotted Frank and his friend sitting outside the restaurant. Frank saw her and waved her over as both men stood up, and Frank introduced her to Merlin. She was immediately struck by his green eyes; long, flowing mane; and modestly covered, well-defined features. She smelled of calla lily, which happened to be Merlin's favorite scent of all; the fragrance instantly brought a memory of his first and only true love. He gallantly took her hand and gently kissed it as though he had been blessed to have an angel in his midst. "It's a distinct pleasure to make your acquaintance, milady. Calla lily is my favorite of exotic flowers."

She looked down in a shy manner, not knowing how to respond. She instantly captured Merlin's heart. Frank, slightly stuttering, broke a moment of uncomfortable silence by thanking Michelle for coming as they all sat down for a bite and a chat. After lunch, Merlin closed his eyes and faced the sun to feel the warmth as Michelle, almost uncontrollably, began to fantasize about moving closer and kissing him. She took a breath and politely said, "So your name is Merlin—just like the magician?"

The amused clone immediately smiled, looked at Frank, and responded, "Yes, just like."

"Excuse me for saying this, but how is it that someone obviously as intelligent as you does not know how to use a computer? To be honest, I was expecting someone much younger, older, or handicapped." Looking slightly embarrassed, she carefully added, "You're not handicapped, are you?"

Merlin laughed at her undeniably sweet charm. Merlin glanced again at Frank and replied, "The reason for that, my angelic tutor, is a very long story."

For the first time in her life, Michelle began searching for her next words, and she finally said, "Okay, when do we start?"

Merlin replied with another smile, "It's already begun."

Frank looked over to Michelle and inquired, "Where are you staying, my dear?"

"On campus—it's the first week of the last term. I can finish that later."

Frank continued, "In that case, please, I insist that you stay with us! We are on a tight schedule, so this temporary arrangement must be full-time, and I assure you, my dear, that you will be well compensated for your time and effort. Who knows? We might even find ourselves on a bit of an adventure along the way."

Father DeCarlo's trusting way put her mind at ease.

"Hey, if we don't take risks, what's the point? Am I right?" Glancing briefly at Merlin, she agreed.

"Brilliant. We have a modest little country inn about one hour out of town; we'll drive to the university first so you can collect your personal effects," the elated Mr. DeCarlo replied. As a show of good faith, he handed her a couple hundred euros.

"I'll have him surfing the net like a seasoned geek in no time."

Frank paid the bill as they headed toward the motorhome and departed for the university campus to collect her things. They arrived at the inn, and Michelle admired the picturesque view. They then promptly showed her to her room to unpack. Michelle got comfortable and freshened up, grabbed her laptop, and met the two men at the kitchen table. "If there are no objections, I thought we might get a jump on things and begin now for an hour or two." Sidling up close to Merlin before they could respond, she opened her laptop and began working slowly as Merlin watched her every move. Frank decided to excuse himself to go out for some fresh air and leave them to it.

"I'll have to assume that you know nothing of what I am about to show you, so please feel free to ask me anything!"

"I'm a quick study and promise to pay close attention," Merlin said, noticing her perfect posture, which accentuated her God-given, angelic shape. Merlin then cleared his throat and slowly said, "You must do this one favor for me, milady: when we are working this close in the future, I would appreciate it if you didn't smell quite so … distracting! I hope you are not offended."

She looked deep into his eyes and sighed. "No, not at all. I understand completely. I should have realized."

Merlin smiled and gently said, "Excellent, then let's begin! The subject de jour is the history of the Freemasons in the United Kingdom. I need to see the names and faces of active key members in this organization."

She immediately began typing and said, "Hmm, interesting subject matter—maybe I'll write a thesis about it." She quickly found a site featuring the United Grand Lodge of England and skimmed past a dry introduction.

> The Masonic Grand Lodge of England fraternity has been suspected of forming much earlier than documented. It was recognized as officially beginning in the year 1717, known then as the Brotherhood of Masonry. They gained popularity when they began to attract people of stature, including royalty, important inventors, wealthy investors, high-ranking politicians, and an extensive lineup of famous entertainers. Unofficially, it's rumored to date back as far as the time of the First Crusade, when the Knights Templar fought to protect the Church. The real catalyst for global recognition began on July 4, 1776, when the Masonic secret society created the Declaration of Independence, written and signed by some of the most influential people of that time, including Thomas Jefferson, John Hancock, Benjamin Franklin, Thomas Paine, George Washington, and others. Together they ushered in the first new world order. Once known as

the Knights of the Brotherhood of Masonry, the group shortened the name to the more familiar Freemasons.

Michelle said, "There doesn't seem to be much in the way of current portraits on this site, but I'll keep looking."

Frank came back in from his short walk.

"Hmm, were either of you aware that you could take a tour through the Masonic museum and library at the great hall in London?"

Both men looked at each other.

"We should go to this Masonic hall if you want to know how it ticks—what better way could there be?"

Frank nodded and said, "Anyone getting hungry? It must be all this clean country air."

After dinner, Merlin, now feeling quite comfortable with the newest recruit, felt compelled to reveal everything to their new friend. About an hour later, after the two men had finished getting her up to speed, Michelle found herself completely speechless. All her traveling and journalistic training could not have prepared her for this situation. She began to wonder how she could possibly accept this incredible story, politely insisting that someone refill her glass immediately. As if in some surreal dream, she gave her head a shake. "A clone of Merlin—the magician from the Dark Ages—on a mission to save the world? Do either of you have any idea how far-fetched that sounds?" She looked at the seriousness on their faces as both men gave her goofy but definitive nods of absolute confirmation. After they answered all of her questions to her satisfaction, Michelle finished her wine and said, "I'm going to go to my room, lock my door, and try to get some sleep, and we'll talk more of this in the morning when we're a bit clearer minded."

Both men agreed and made themselves ready for bed, confident that their newest member would see the light in the morning. Morning arrived, and a more open-minded Michelle lay in her bed, thinking, *If this is true, then as a journalist, I am compelled to look upon this as a once-in-a-lifetime adventure. How could I do otherwise?* Without skipping a beat, she got up and made breakfast for the boys before they set out for the long drive ahead, much to the delight of Frank and Merlin. They all climbed into the camper and headed to London. Michelle, at this point, was convinced that these men were harmless to her and decided to be on guard, have a bit of faith, and see what happened. Merlin took a break as he charged his Bluetooth device the professor had provided and plugged it into the port just behind his ear. He accessed the music library, inserted his earbuds, and began listening to vintage blues; he was immediately hooked on the sounds of guitars. Once a seasoned player of the lute back in his day, he quickly learned to appreciate and absorb a variety of genres.

Michelle said, "I am beginning to believe that there's a story here—let me stay and write about it! I can also help out. I'll shop for groceries, cook, clean—anything you need—and when it's over, I'll go back to where you found me. Deal?"

Frank responded, "I'm sorry, my dear, but this is one story that cannot be told."

With puppy-dog eyes and pouty lips, she stared at Merlin. He thought for a minute, nodded, and said, "We've told you everything there is to sway you into being one of us; we need your help. You can stay and make your notes, but it may only be made public as fiction, and that, milady, is nonnegotiable."

She agreed to this unusual journey, smiled, hugged them both from behind, and did her happy dance, causing the two men to laugh.

Nearing midday, they entered the heart of London, where the great Masonic lodge sat. Michelle soon noticed a sign saying Freemasons Hall Library and Museum. They parked across the street, paid the entrance fee, and walked into the building, where they saw rare books, artifacts, documents, and artwork from every era. Merlin began to feel like a proud father looking over some of their accomplishments. The elated Merlin closed his eyes, took a deep breath, and, unbeknownst to him, began to slightly levitate two inches above the ground. A frightened little boy next to him saw this and ran away screaming. Michelle started taking pictures of everything on display.

One of the security guards eagerly gave her a private tour as she continued to take notes and pictures, including several of the guard. An hour after, Merlin detected the unmistakable scent of calla lily again as Michelle moved up close behind him and softly whispered in his ear, "Merlin, I've collected everything I could—what's next?"

He suddenly experienced a tingling sensation that spread from his ears to his feet, as if a spell had been cast upon him. A warm, familiar feeling surged throughout his body, reminding him immediately of his one true love, the Lady of Shalott, who had bathed exclusively using the same exotic flower. He turned around, and they stared deeply into each other's eyes for a few seconds that seemed to slow or even stop time for them both, as if everyone in the room had disappeared. They broke each other's gaze to get Frank's attention and head back to the camper, armed with all the information they had found. They had to find something that could help change the direction of the dark path the Masons were apparently on. At the wheel, Frank recommended that they check in to a nearby hotel to save time. Michelle also suggested that they stop and shop for previsions. They agreed, and soon after, they all stepped inside a large department store that seemed to have everything under one roof. Merlin instantly gravitated toward the musical-instrument area and became awestruck by the guitars on display. He sat down and began playing a high-end Martin acoustic model that he quickly adjusted to and enjoyed greatly as he entertained a couple of children. Impressed at the level of Merlin's playing, Frank happily bought the guitar for his talented friend. Merlin looked up at the appointed one and said, "A lute never sounded this good."

With bags full of stuff, they left the store. Michelle then asked Frank whether or not Merlin had proper identification.

"Not as of yet, I'm afraid."

Michelle responded, "It just so happens that I know a guy who knows a guy who can do that and lives right here in town, last I heard. He's going to need a birth certificate, passport, and driver's license. I'll make the call."

Frank looked up to apologize to God in advance, focused on Merlin, and replied, "He is twenty-four years of age, is from South Wales, and goes by the name of Martin DeCarlo, my youngest brother. Thank you, my dear—please arrange it, whatever the cost!"

Chapter 8

The UGLE is the governing body of Freemasonry throughout the United Kingdom. Beneath this mysterious structure lay a covert command center set up in the subbasement of the great Masonic hall, run exclusively by Seth, appointed by Gabriel for his military intelligence and blackened heart. The facility included direct uplinks from Interpol's mainframe, using the Echelon network surveillance, giving them a front-row seat to everything Big Brother saw and heard anywhere in Europe. Also at his disposal is a well-trained small group of dedicated, low-profile mercenaries with access to specially designed land, sea, and air vehicles with stealth-mode capabilities—originally arranged for the Masonic organization's security needs as Gabriel and Seth saw fit and with the government's blessings and unofficial seal of approval.

Upstairs in the main office, Gabriel reached deep into his private wall safe and removed a small, narrow lead box. It had long been rumored to contain a message written at the time of the Crusades, finally ready to be opened and read. The etching on the ancient object was addressed to the grand master of 2013, but Gabriel had always been defiant of any authority. He thought that at the very least, it would make a fine addition to their museum.

With great anticipation, he felt like a child about rip open a long-awaited, wrapped Christmas gift. Gabriele immediately summoned his right-hand man, Seth, and a few of his highest-ranking brothers to witness the long-anticipated event behind closed doors. Brother Joshua brought a small, portable drill and a hacksaw, as instructed by Gabriel, for the content extraction. He carefully pierced the thin casing with a small hole in one end, allowing for a fiber-optic video camera to safely look inside the ancient mystery box. When Gabriel exposed a well-preserved wooden box with the Masonic emblem carved on its surface, everyone was surprised, especially Gabriel. Gabriel then used the small hacksaw to carefully cut an inch off the end, slowly tilting the wooden box as it slid out of its ancient lead tomb and into the large, waiting hand of Gabriel. He carefully opened the box and removed a rolled-up sheet of parchment, which was in surprisingly good condition. He unfurled the paper and, with an uncharacteristic look of disbelief, read the ancient text aloud to his brothers as they all leaned forward with anticipation.

> Greetings, my knightly brothers. I trust this letter
> finally found its way to you. Gentlemen, what you
> are about to hear might be difficult to believe,
> but believe you must, for it is the sworn word of
> a humble man with no cause to lie. I write this
> letter to you from the year 1099. My good friend
> the pope approves and supports the first crusade to
> Jerusalem. On rare quiet evenings, ghostly echoes
> of screaming battles are heard, won and lost—an
> ongoing cycle of brutal madness, leaving bloody
> trails of dismembered bodies, despair, and disease
> in their ruthless wakes. Fortunately, I was spared

from most of the horror during the darkest of days. Certain knowledge and talents of mine have afforded me special favor with some of the most influential people of this era. I am the creator of the Brotherhood of the Knights of Masonry. Pope Urban II granted me six of his best knights to serve and keep me safe for the rest of my journey on this earth. It was my intent to maintain the knightly bloodlines of my guardians-turned-master-masons and truest brothers. It was agreed by all to keep my identity secret because I could only be a diversion, having been blessed with a few talents, including possessing the ability to see distant future events. I have proudly seen you flourish into the most powerful organization filled with honorable men, far surpassing my expectations, and I am proud to have been the spark that lit the flame. However, there is currently an evil presence among you that must be discovered before it's too late. Good luck, my brothers.

As above, so below, M.

A confused and unsettling pause loomed over the surreal moment as Gabriel looked at the dumbfounded knights. With surprisingly catlike quickness, he took control and squeezed out an award-winning laugh, giving the impression that it was a hoax he had carefully orchestrated. "You should see the looks on your faces!" he said, adding another forced chuckle. "Gentlemen, I apologize for the deception; you must excuse my warped sense of humor!

I thought that a bit of levity would make for a refreshing change around here—did it not?"

Recognizing Gabriel as being out of character, the knights responded with a mixture of laughter and relief. Gabriel sighed, and a bead of sweat rolled down his temple as he placed the letter in the wooden box and slid it back into the lead casing. "Now, my brothers, it's time to move on to more current and serious matters."

This episode didn't sit well with Joshua, as he was more than a bit suspicious, though Gabriel didn't seem to take notice. Two hours later, the meeting was adjourned, and they filed out of the room. Gabriel had Seth hang back for a private chat. Still amused with Gabriel's little prank, Seth noticed the concerned seriousness in Gabriel's face and quickly leveled off. Gabriel whispered, "I don't for a minute believe that letter, but in the unlikely event that it is in any way remotely authentic, I want you to keep a close eye on anything suspicious! Use your specialized resources to find out who this M could possibly be! Also, I want you to keep a close eye on Brother Joshua—am I clear?"

Appearing a bit confused, Seth replied, "Yes, of course, my lord. I'll get on that right away." Down in the control room, Seth began his search; he leaned into his monitor, looking at video feeds from in and around the great hall from the past few days. A couple of hours later, with his head cradled in one hand and a mouse in the other, just as his now-heavy eyelids began to give way to the forces of gravity, Seth watched a crowd of people in the museum, when something caught his attention. He noticed a man seemingly rise a couple of inches from the floor for a few seconds before coming back down again. He immediately rubbed his eyes to readjust his focus and thought that the man must have been standing on his toes. He then noticed the frightened face of a little boy standing beside him; the boy looked down to where the man was standing, looked up, and quickly ran away. Seth watched the scene several times, convinced that something was not right. Soon after, a woman approached the man in the video and called another man, and they all left together. His instincts caused him to get suspicious, and he decided to target these three to be found for an interrogation.

Chapter

9

Later that afternoon, Merlin's friends found a cozy local inn just outside of London to stay in temporarily. Frank and Michelle both headed out to get some pizza and wine. Now alone, Merlin decided to enjoy a long, hot shower and an hour of blissful meditation. Merlin's friends arrived back at the inn with dinner, and Michelle quietly walked through the door backward, holding a large pepperoni pizza. As she turned around, she was immediately stunned to see Merlin floating in the lotus position, just above the floor, in front of a lit fireplace, wearing nothing more than a pair of briefs and a T-shirt under an oversized hooded black bathrobe. She froze from the shock of the unreal scene before her. Frank arrived at the door, and they both looked at each other to validate the surreal moment with wide eyes and dropped jaws. Michelle slowly moved closer in disbelief, tripped on the edge of the rug, and fell to the floor.

The sound caused Merlin to snap out of his meditative trance, and he chuckled at his friends' reactions. Frank closed his eyes, dropped to his knees, and began praying. Merlin got up, gently picked Michelle up off the floor, and placed her on the couch as he began to laugh again. Confused and embarrassed, Michelle apologized for the unusually awkward display. "That whole floating trick thing just freaked me out. I'm all right."

"Forgive me for startling you, my friends, but that was not an illusion," he exclaimed. "I have just regained one of my cosmic gifts: I happen to defy gravity whenever I meditate or just feel at peace. You are the only friends I have in this world, and I do humbly apologize for frightening you—please forgive me!"

The shaken priest drew a deep breath as if he had been holding it since he walked in, and he said, "Okay, okay, but if your head begins to spin about, I'm on the next plane back to the Vatican."

They all enjoyed a good laugh as Merlin rubbed his neck, trying to imagine what that unpleasant experience might feel like. "What is that intoxicatingly aromatic scent?" Michelle blushed, thinking that he was referring to her perfume.

Frank sniffed the air and said, "We call it pizza; take a slice and enjoy." They all ate while Frank and Michelle desperately tried to adjust to and accept their new friend's unusual talent.

After the meal, Merlin poured himself another glass of wine. "Two things: first, that pizza was exceptional, and second, I am the least person you need fear—please believe me." They convincingly smiled and nodded together.

"Do people still enjoy a good magic trick, or is that considered an extinct form of entertainment in this world?" Michelle replied.

"Oh, it's still very much alive and well all over the world, and if I'm not mistaken, it's mostly all thanks to you."

Like a couple of kids just given an extra hour before bedtime, Frank and Michelle both smiled and snuggled back on the couch. Beginning to feel like his old young self again, Merlin quickly drew the curtains, allowing only the calm but steady firelight to set the stage. He then lit a large candle in front of his private audience and theatrically stood and turned his body around to face the warmth emanating from the pulsating embers. He raised his hood over his head, turned around, and moved up close to face the fire. He stretched out his arms, chanting a few chilling words in Latin as they saw only his larger-than-life frame in front of a well-lit fire. He clenched his fists and then suddenly released his fingers outward toward the flames; sparks seemed to fly off his fingertips. The calm fire suddenly spiked into a blinding flash, and Frank and Michelle were now on the edges of their seats with anticipation. A few seconds ticked by in silence as Merlin's large dark robe stood motionless in the dancing firelight. Frank and Michelle again looked at each other in complete confusion, and Michelle said, "I don't get it—where's the magic in that? Don't be embarrassed, Merlin; you're probably just out of practice."

Michelle finally got up and stepped forward to touch Merlin's shoulder. As she did, the robe collapsed without Merlin in it, leaving her holding up the robe as she frantically looked around the room and then right at Frank. "That's messed up. I mean, how is that even possible?"

Just then, they heard a gentle knock at the front door. Wearing his jeans and a big smile, Merlin walked right in. Speechless at first, in awe, they stood up and applauded the most impressive magic act either of them had ever seen. Merlin again smiled, put his robe back on, bowed nobly, and sat down on the couch. "In a long-since-forgotten world of darkness, I have done battle with the devil and could have easily been killed on more than one occasion along the way, but I was spared. Evil is a cancer that must be removed at all costs, and if need be, people must die trying. There is a malignant tumor deep within the body of my creation, and it has fallen to me to extract and expose it. Satan has emerged to play again, but then, so have I, and we shall do battle—but this time, I have help, and his days are numbered. Most of my visions were of this world many centuries ago, but recently, I witnessed my first near-future event.

"There is a plot to assassinate the grand master and take over a large part of the world, so our task is to intercept the attempt and expose the evil men involved." He paused again with a grin. "I am unlike any human before me that I am aware of, and you must get beyond that fact if we are to succeed."

They sat in silence for a while, with only the calming sound of a crackling fire; then they yawned almost simultaneously and all burst out into laughter as they prepared to sleep. That night, in his room, Merlin lit a candle, removed the map from his book, and began reading. The next morning calmly arrived, and a wide-awake Michelle asked the men to join her in the diner across the street for breakfast; they happily complied. As the content trio lingered over coffee, Merlin said, "There is something I must retrieve, and it's several hours away. I'll explain on the way, but first, we're going to need provisions, such as tools, some rope, and a blanket."

Soon they were on an empty road in the country with their required supplies and Merlin carefully behind the wheel. Enjoying the drive immensely, he told his friends of his golden statue, hoping that it was still sealed in the cave so that they might use it as a decoy to help divert attention from themselves. Typing quickly on her laptop, Michelle took notes, desperately trying not to miss any sequence of events as they happened. An hour into the trip, Michelle went through the images of the Masonic exhibit on a slide show on her laptop as Frank leaned forward from the backseat to get a better view. Trying not to get too distracted as he drove, Merlin glanced at her computer and abruptly pulled the vehicle over to the shoulder. "I've seen this man before—who is he?" said Merlin.

Michelle replied, "It says that his name is Sir Gabriel Hammond III; he's the current pro grand master, second only to the honorable grand master himself, Prince Hayden Trask. His primary responsibilities are to oversee the entire UK region from his office in the legendary Masonic hall in the UK."

With a stern conviction, Merlin said, "He is the evil I spoke of and must be removed from his office."

Frank said, "Merlin, my friend, your passion is as compelling as it is infectious, but you do remember that I am a man of God and cannot condone the taking of a life."

"No offense, Father, but if God is really there, then he better know that taking one life to ensure the safety of hundreds or thousands of people is justification for survival," said Michelle.

"My dear, sweet girl, faith made it real, and it will be by his hand, not ours. We are merely expendable pawns in a much larger game of chess."

A long, silent gap of time blanketed the moment as Merlin began to formulate their best course of action. Still eyeing the images, she added, "They all look like a group of stuffed shirts to me."

"Stuffed shirts?" Merlin replied.

"People who are all business and no play," Frank replied.

"Ah, yes, of course—stuffed shirts. That's fitting." Merlin began to tire after a few hours, and Frank took the wheel, with Merlin now riding shotgun. The reborn demigod continued his research by activating his internal computer implant and began to absorb volumes of the history of the known universe, wearing an expression of awe, at an almost superhuman rate of speed. They soon arrived at their destination: the closest point from the highway to Merlin's old crystal cave at the edge of the rainforest. Using his Bluetooth, Merlin accessed the video screen system that projected a satellite mapping image of the area. They grabbed their provisions and began their hike down into the heart of the rainforest. After an hour through rugged terrain, Frank and Michelle sat to catch their breath on a large rock. Unbeknownst to them, they were at their destination—just in front of the wall of water by the cave. Merlin told them to wait there as he gingerly walked over the loose rocks that lay just in front of the cave behind the sparkling waterfall. Vines and thick foliage appeared to have interlocked themselves across the stone-covered mouth, virtually creating a completely undetectable secret vault.

Suddenly, a large shadow appeared from directly above them and completely blocked the sunlight. A silent black helicopter with no markings landed in a nearby clearing, and five men dressed in military uniforms, led by Seth, exited the craft and flashed their credentials. "Interpol! Stop what you are doing, and raise your hands in the air!" The men quickly converged on the startled crusaders as Merlin came out from behind the liquid curtain. Seth drew and pointed his custom-made ceramic pistol in Merlin's direction, spewing out commands with a condescending tone. It quickly occurred to Seth that they were unarmed, and he lowered his weapon.

The seasoned priest responded, "You have no cause to be here; we are not breaking any law."

Seth sternly replied, "Well, my Italian friend, what may appear obvious to some only seems that way because that's the way it was made to look."

Frank turned to Michelle and whispered, "Is it just me, or was that complete gibberish?" She nervously laughed.

"It's my job to detain anyone of interest, and you three stooges are currently that. Last week, you were all seen together at the Masonic hall museum."

Seth swiftly moved right up to Merlin, getting nose to nose, and said, "I saw you levitate clean off the floor—how was that achieved?"

"I simply think happy thoughts."

Clearly upset, Seth raised his voice. "I want to see some identification, and while I wait for that, I want to know what you three are doing here!"

Merlin replied, "We are simply exploring this majestic forest—why bother us?"

Seth snarled back, "Oh, I do apologize—am I bothering you? Perhaps I should go away and come back at a more convenient time."

Merlin sarcastically responded, "If you wouldn't mind, my good man—we're on a very tight schedule," adding a wink and a smile of confidence.

Shocked at first and then quickly turning rather amused, Seth let out a laugh, almost appearing to be admiring Merlin's spirit. Seth got a closer look at the tools they were carrying. "What could you possibly be looking for in the middle of nowhere— buried treasure?" Seth pointed to Merlin and yelled out to his men, "This one was behind the waterfall—check it out!"

The men went in with machetes and pry bars, and they hacked away on the vines; the others saw blade tips bobbing through the wall of water with every thrust. A few minutes later, rocks and small boulders rolled out through the waterfall. Seth then hissed, "It's my job to make sure people are safe—well, are you safe?"

Merlin paused and then replied, "It doesn't feel that way—is that a trick question?"

Frank and Michelle both produced their identification, and Merlin acted as if he had innocently lost his. Just then, they heard a commotion coming from behind the cascade of water. Seth moved quickly into the cave. He was surprised to see the walls completely lined in crystal, but what took his breath away was a large statue of a golden dragon with beautifully set clusters of diamonds in its teeth, talons, and tail, and two large rubies for its eyes. Seth was so excited to see this priceless treasure that he paid almost no attention to the unmarked stone coffin that lay beside it. The men soon come out from behind the water wall, carrying something large and heavy wrapped in a black cloth. They carefully loaded the shrouded object into the backseat of the helicopter as its engine slowly began to power up. Seth asked Merlin, "How did you know there was something buried here?"

Merlin pulled out his map and said, "I found this map and followed it here." Completing the performance, Merlin added, "You've just stolen my property."

Seth snatched the map from Merlin's grasp, pulled out a walkie-talkie, and ordered his men to park his Hummer right behind the motorhome located on the main road and wait for them to arrive.

He then drew his pistol. "A nobody with no identification could easily end up dead and sealed inside a well-hidden cave if you three breathe a word to anyone about this." He added with a condescending tone, "Do you understand, Mr. Nobody?" "I'm going to hold you three for questioning—now move!" Seth and the pilot climbed into the chopper while his detainees were escorted back out to the main highway. Once they reached the road, they were told to get into the back of the large black Hummer.

Inside the vehicle, Frank said, "I would like to know how they found us so quickly. They're either very lucky, very good, or a bit of both." Slightly panic-stricken, Michelle began to hyperventilate, triggering Frank to start praying in a frantic whisper.

Merlin attempted to calm them both down by slapping his hands together, grabbing their attention, and saying, "I want the two of you to breathe deeply, sit back, and clear your minds. We are guppies in an ocean of much bigger fish; have no fear, and trust in me!" He guided them into a much calmer place as they began breathing in sync, deeper and deeper. As all three sat back and breathed deeply with eyes closed in complete silence, Merlin smiled and began to softly sing. "Don't worry about a thing, 'cause every little thing's going to be all right."

Frank and Michelle both smiled and instantly forgot where they were for the moment. A knockout gas was then released into the back compartment, quickly rendering the captives unconscious. In a clearing by the side of the road, Seth exited the helicopter and said, "Put the girl and the old man inside the camper! Keep the unknown man in the truck, and meet me at the mobile base unit just outside Leeds around midnight for interrogation! There's something about this guy, and I intend to find out what it is." Seth then rushed back toward the waiting chopper, whose blades were in motion, and climbed into the backseat with his magnificent treasure. Up in the air, Seth muttered to himself with excitement as he touched the statue, "Gabriel's not going to believe what I've got for him."

When he arrived back at the great hall, he presented it to an elated Gabriel. Hours later, Frank and Michelle both woke up groggy with two big headaches, but they were safe in their motorhome. By then, night had fallen upon them, so they decided to wait until morning to set out to find their friend. Late that night, somewhere outside of Leeds, Merlin began to regain consciousness; he opened his eyes and found himself tied securely to a cold metal chair, bound at the wrists, waist, and ankles under a bright light in a dark room. He recalled seeing the scene briefly in a dream vision. Still in a bit of a fog, he gave his head a shake. "Why am I here, and while I'm at it, what have you done with my friends?"

"They've been released—unharmed. If I were you, I'd be more concerned about your situation and try to prevent any unnecessary unpleasantness from occurring. What do you know of the object we took from the cave?"

"Nothing. Like I told you, I found a map and followed it— that's it!"

"Okay, so where did you find the map?"

"Hidden inside an old book I found."

"You and your friends were seen at the Masonic museum last week, and you all seemed excessively curious—and that made me curious too. Why is that? You're either spies or just Freemason junkies on an adventure, so which is it?"

"I'm sorry—I wasn't listening. Could you repeat the choices?"

Seth let out a laugh. "You have sand, my son—I'll give you that. From time to time, I am called upon to locate and identify certain people of interest, and right now, I find you quite interesting thus far. I can't quite put my finger on it, but there's something about you that's just not right."

Merlin grinned and responded, "It's late, and you seem to be experiencing something of a conundrum. Perhaps have a hot cup of tea—it's a hug in a mug."

Amused, Seth gave an evil leer. "I'm not known as a very patient man, and that will not work in your favor, I'm afraid. I'm quite good at what I do, so if I were you, I'd be completely compliant!" With his patience quickly diminishing, Gabriel's watchdog got nose to nose with Merlin. "You don't appear to be scared—you really should be, you know!"

Merlin, now becoming a bit weary and inpatient himself, said, "If I displayed fear, would that help speed things up some?"

Realizing that his detainee did not intend to cooperate, Seth decided to move on to other means of interrogation at his disposal. A bit perplexed, Seth took a step back and surprised Merlin, pushing a button that sent high amounts of electrical current surging into his body for a few seconds. Seth said with a trembling voice, "Was that good for you?" After that surprising, painful experience, Merlin uncontrollably shed a tear. Seth then yelled, "Who are you?"

A sigh and a brave smirk were all Merlin had for the new-world warlord. Completely frustrated, Seth pressed the button a second time, sending even higher volts of electricity through Merlin for a much longer time than before. A full two minutes passed, which seemed an eternity of torture to Merlin. Taking every ounce of strength he possessed, Merlin successfully appeared to remain unfazed and defiant as he fought off the pain, smiling into the blinding light.

"You have thus far been strong and brave," Seth said softly, creeping up behind Merlin. "But we have hours, and I'm just getting warmed up." Immensely enjoying the moment, the sadistic madman hit the button a third time without another word. Then, as Seth went to push the button again, suddenly, the only light in the room, which was pointed directly at Merlin's face, went black.

Seth panicked, searching for a light, when he was quickly knocked out and hit the floor hard as Merlin escaped out the back door. Seth soon regained consciousness and stumbled about; he turned on the main light switch, finding no prisoner in the room. Seth checked to see if his jaw had been broken and then quickly exited the interrogation room. Frantically looking around, he called out to his driver to help find his prisoner. Pounding his fist on the trailer wall, feeling cheated out of his only real pleasure, he screamed, "The next time we meet, we're going to dispense with the foreplay."

Merlin took to the nearby trees by the road, where he waited quietly for the truck to leave and eventual daybreak. He remembered the last time he had been compelled to hide in a forest and began to silently cry for the comfort of his mother's arms and reassuring words.

Chapter

10

Early the next morning, in the camper, Michelle and Frank attempted to clear their heads and ascertain where Merlin might have been taken. "He could be anywhere; we have to find him soon as humanly possible!" Just then, Frank remembered Merlin's homing device implanted by the institute. He called the professor's cell phone and woke him up, saying that he and HC13 had been separated and that he needed to locate him right away. After fumbling about for a minute, the professor told him that Merlin appeared to be stationary off the main road in a forest just outside of Leeds. Frank thanked the professor, grabbed the wheel, and sped southward toward Leeds, praying along the way. Frank determined that if Merlin was in a forest, he was either hiding or dead, and he began to pray again for his good friend's life.

Finally, after a couple of long, anxious hours, Michelle spotted a figure walking on the shoulder of the main road, heading toward them. "There he is—that's him!"

Frank pulled right up to Merlin, and Michelle jumped out of the vehicle just before it came to a complete stop. She ran directly over to him and gave an exhausted Merlin a big hug, which he had needed desperately. His friends helped him into the vehicle and onto one of the beds, where he collapsed from exhaustion. "Are you in need of medical attention, my friend?"

"Nothing that a shower, sleep, and shave—in any order— won't cure."

They all shared a short laugh as Merlin lost consciousness. Frank decided to go back to their country inn to regroup and plan their next move. The next morning, the sun shone brightly on the little inn as a refreshed Merlin exited a long, hot shower to get ready for the new day. The fresh smell of coffee and bacon alerted the men that it was time to begin the day. They all gathered around the breakfast table for the morning meal Michelle had graciously prepared. "We have only just begun our quest, and already you have saved my life more than once. I'm afraid that I may never be able to repay you both."

"Successfully completing our mission safely would be more than enough payment for us, my friend," Frank humbly replied. Merlin shed his second tear in the new world.

With an unreachable itch in his mind, Seth called for an emergency meeting with his shadow patrol unit. He ordered his men to patrol the perimeter and keep an eye out for anything suspiciously threatening to the central London area, and one motorhome in particular. "If this vehicle is found, report it to me immediately!" Specially modified transportation provided by the military included one Hummer, two motorcycles, one tractor trailer, and a helicopter. All were black and unmarked, with darkly tinted windows and silent-mode engines for covert operations. The men all complied and exited to their assigned vehicles. Directly linked into Interpol's mainframe, Seth conducted his search for his escaped prisoner by way of audio and video that included high-security intel from all over Europe.

Back at the inn, after breakfast, Merlin conveyed an idea. "If we knew the grand master's travel plans, we could meet with him face-to-face. It may be our only real chance."

Frank shrugged and said, "Sure, and right after that, they'll have us all arrested and declared legally insane, whether we are or not."

A silent pause filled the room. Merlin nodded and then calmly replied, "It's a gamble—I grant you that—and we're betting with our lives. If we don't try, we'll never know—and know we must!"

Michelle opened her laptop and began searching for the Masonic grand master's schedule. In almost no time at all, she said, "Here it is; I have his itinerary. It says that he will be here in London at the great hall next Saturday for their annual meeting and dinner event."

"Excellent, we will also require someone on the inside working with us. He must be an honorable, high-ranking knight or assistant willing to conspire against his brothers."

"Can an honorable man spy against his own family?"

"If a member is suspected of being evil, let us hope so!"

In the cafeteria of the great hall, Grand Secretary Joshua began eating lunch. He was soon met by his boss, the pro grand master, Brother Gabriel. "Joshua, I haven't had a chance to talk to you about our last meeting—what did you think?"

Joshua put some food in his mouth just before Gabriel finished, to stall for the best answer he could offer. After a few good chews, he swallowed and took a gulp of his coffee to wash down a rather dry chicken sandwich. He then filled his lungs and cleared his throat. "I thought that it was informative and rather entertaining."

As if trying to decipher Joshua's response, Gabriel squinted and, with an unsettled tone, tilted his head, leaned toward Joshua, and said, "You're referring to my little prank, yes?"

"Why, yes, of course, Brother; it was quite cleverly executed right down to the mysterious M."

Gabriel was not quite sure how to interpret that response, so he smiled and leaned forward as he said, "I played you all using an ancient prophecy of our pending doom in the year 2013 or something like that. All I had to do was create a suitable prop with a message and store it for three years. It was really more for my own amusement."

Now completely convinced of Gabriel's guilt, all Joshua could do was say, "Very well played, Brother—masterfully done." The good knight's body froze with fear as a cold shiver ran up his spine. He had always prided himself on being a good judge of character—until now, that was.

Up in his office, Gabriel had a private chat with his number one. As Gabriel towered over the smaller-framed Seth, he sternly said, "Brother, you are my eyes and ears, and for us to be successful, you must remain on point and not dwell in a failed abduction, especially over a nobody! How do the Americans put it? We have bigger fish to fry. Next week, our brother the grand master will be here for the annual meeting, and I want you to see to it that everything goes according to plan. I've worked too hard for too long, and I will not tolerate any more distractions. The grand master's seat will soon finally be mine. Should anything distract you from your duties, you will be escorted from this building, shot, bagged, and dropped into to the bottom of the river, understand?"

Seth cowered and humbly agreed. "Yes, my lord—clearly."

Frank returned the camper to the rental outlet and went to another dealer for a newer model as they continued on their way back to London. Michelle became inspired. "My father used to say that the best fruit is always found on the vine. Although he was referring to his vineyard and meant that literally, the same rule still applies here! With our new vehicle and license plate, what safer place could there be but in front of the Masonic hall? That may be the safest and last place they would expect us to be."

The two men looked at each other as if to say, *Why didn't we think of that?* and nodded in compliance.

Michelle added, "We'll need some specialized equipment, like binoculars, a parabolic microphone, and some luck."

The next morning, they found an inconspicuous place to park with a clear view of the entrance of the UGLE. From behind their tinted rear window, they watched well-dressed men entering the large fortress and noticed several video cameras strategically placed around the perimeter. Her heart raced with excitement at participating in her first real stakeout; she sensed a potential adventure just ahead.

It wasn't long before she spotted a kind-faced, well-dressed gentleman and went to her list of key personnel on her computer. She quickly matched the honest-looking man with the subheading of Grand Secretary Sir Joshua Rigby. "He does have a trustworthy look about him, don't you think?" Michelle began gathering all the information available on their possible newest member.

Joshua entered his office, which was situated near Gabriel's. He soon heard the unusual sound of someone faintly whispering—something Gabriel was not exactly known for. Already suspicious of Gabriel's motives, Joshua decided to carefully listen in on another extension, and he heard an upset Gabriel softly but clearly say to Seth, "Yes, I know what I said—I was the one who said it.

It occurred to me that an unknown, resourceful person practically knocking on our door and wanting to know all about you and I during such a pivotal time—not to mention the appearance of that letter—equals trouble, and we must not have any of that now, must we? We are to take no more chances—not now. How do you know he wanted to know about us specifically, Brother?"

"I was told that one of the museum security guards just happened to mention it casually in the cafeteria over coffee and a muffin."

"I want this man found again and brought to me in good health—is that clear?"

"Yes, my lord—crystal."

The disturbed grand secretary carefully hung up the phone.

Out front, Merlin reminded his friends that despite having unlimited financial funding from the Church, they had to remain cautious and focused. "Until we have leverage to expose and extract the madmen masquerading as honorable knights, we must exercise caution. I am reminded of something an ancient priest once told me: on the coldest of winter nights, all living things must find warmth or die, even if it means thawing inside the opened jaws of a sleeping dragon. In other words, the closer we get, the more invisible we are to become."

Midday approached, and Merlin's possible prospect, Sir Joshua, exited the building, casually chatting with the door attendant, seemingly on his way out to lunch. The attendant said, "Good day, Sir Joshua."

"Good day to you, Sir Archie." As he bowed, they shared a bit of a laugh together.

"Evil men don't usually take the time to chat and laugh with the hired help—that's our man," Merlin said to the appointed one. "Brother, you are the obvious choice to make first contact, and hopefully we will gain his confidence quickly. Feel him out first before you get to it! He could easily sic Seth and his minions on us in a heartbeat with one phone call. Do not be overanxious or too casual!"

Sir Joshua headed on foot toward a pub that he frequented across the street, much to the delight of Merlin and company as they looked on. The knight found a small table outside and requested a plate of fish and chips with a pint of Guinness black lager from the waitress. Mulling over what he had previously heard at the office, he shook his head in disbelief, trying to make sense of it all. Frank approached the pub, walked up to Joshua's table, and kindly introduced himself.

"A pleasure to meet you, sir. I am—"

The ex-priest politely interrupted him to say, "Sir Joshua Rigby, the Freemasons' grand secretary of the UK and the youngest to ever be knighted by the queen. Known to all as a loyal and well-respected servant of the highest order."

Appearing a bit stunned, Joshua replied, "I'm afraid you have me at a disadvantage, sir—have we met?"

"Please excuse my boldness; we have never met, good sir, but I know of you." Immediately convinced that this was indeed a man to trust, Frank dove right in. "I am Father Frank DeCarlo, a priest from Rome."

"If that is so, then where is your Roman collar, and why are you dressed in common street clothes?"

"It's a rather strange story, but I beg of you to hear me out first before you make any decisions!" An intrigued Joshua nodded and listened as Frank began to explain himself. "The condensed version is, I was ordered by His Holiness to find a book that sent me on a journey to expose an evil that leads directly to your door." Twenty minutes later, with Joshua's profound attention, Frank concluded by telling him of an evil presence now leading the Freemasons into a time of uncertainty and chaos.

After all he had seen and heard thus far from Gabriel and Seth, Joshua was inclined to believe the possibility of what this priest was saying. "If this is true—and I'm not saying it is—what would you have me do?"

Now feeling a bit more confident, Frank replied, "I'm glad you asked; we believe that the fate of the free world may well rest in your hands."

Joshua politely replied, "Okay, and who exactly are 'we'?"

"Another good question. There is someone with me who can explain everything better than I, but first, I need to know if we can trust you. Can we?"

With a reassuring look, Joshua replied, "I am nothing, sir, if not honorable. Okay, you've piqued my curiosity—where is this friend of yours?"

"He is in the motorhome just across the way."

The good knight finished his lunch, paid the check, and walked with Frank toward the vehicle. Michelle opened the camper door wide to greet them with a welcoming wave and smile. Joshua looked at Frank, took a deep breath, and cautiously stepped up into the vehicle, where he saw Merlin seated at the far side of the table. Michelle made the timely introductions, and Merlin shook Joshua's hand and politely requested that they all be seated. The cautious Mason complied with a certain degree of apprehension; his eyes darted around, searching for some kind of hidden video-recording device. There was no sign of anything of that nature.

Joshua looked up and said, "Merlin as in the magician Merlin of Camelot?"

"King Arthur of Camelot lived over a century before I was born. The history book scribes placed us in the same era to make a more well-rounded story, I suppose." Merlin allowed a few moments of silence.

Then Joshua stood and said, "It's a pleasure to meet you, and I am the queen of England."

Merlin laughed as he replied, "Please indulge me and give me just ten minutes of your valuable time, good sir! After that, if you are still not convinced, I will thank you for your time and we shall never speak again."

"So let me get this straight—you're going to try to convince me that you have returned from the dead to save the world?" Joshua shook his head and laughed. "The floor is yours."

Merlin glanced down to the floor and smiled. Thirty minutes later, a befuddled Joshua was still listening carefully to the story. Merlin went on to explain how he and his friends had been detained and abducted by someone named Seth from Interpol. It didn't take long for the high-ranking Freemason to become completely convinced. After hearing the story, as Frank had done, he too decided to go on a bit of faith. Joshua squinted and tilted his head, suddenly reminded of an unusual phone conversation between Gabriel, his boss, and the second-in-command, Seth. "This can't be a coincidence! Just this morning, I overheard my boss, Gabriel, the pro grand master, tell the deputy grand master, Seth, to find an escaped detainee for more questioning." Looking at Merlin, Joshua said, "Let me guess—you?"

Merlin nodded. "Is there anything else?"

Joshua shook his head from side to side and then recalled Gabriel's letter. "Last week, Gabriel read an unusual letter to six of the highest-ranking knights that stunned everyone in the room. Yet after reading it, Gabriel claimed to have written it himself for his own amusement. It seemed obvious only to myself that he was lying.

"I can't recite it verbatim, but I can tell you that it looked ancient and was eloquently stated, and the author was the founder of the Knights of the Brotherhood of Masonry. It went on to say that he was also a prophet and spoke of an evil presence currently in charge, and it was mysteriously signed with the letter *M*."

Merlin began reciting the letter word for word exactly as it had been written. All the good knight could do was shake his head in disbelief and say, "Then the *M* stands for Merlin?"

Merlin and his friends all nodded.

"I'm going to need some time to process all this."

"Of course, Brother." Frank and Michelle openly admitted to grappling with the reality that he was a perfect copy of the legendary Merlin, to help Joshua come to terms with it.

With a serious expression, Joshua said, "Okay, you've convinced me, but again, how can I help?"

Merlin told the good knight he was convinced that the grand master was going to be assassinated by Gabriel for complete control. "He must be stopped by any means possible before this event occurs, or many people will suffer with this madman on the loose. I planted the Masonic seed; it is connected to me by the root, so it comes down to us. We need someone on the inside; we need a spy."

Joshua paused and drew a deep breath as he attempted to wrap his head around the moment. He got up, stepped away from the table, and knelt down in front of Merlin. "If I can help make a difference for good in this world, then my services are in your charge with all my heart, my lord."

Merlin knelt down to face Joshua. "I am no one's master. I am a man on a mission who is desperate to maintain the integrity of the Masonic fraternity." He then added, "Thank you, Sir Joshua, my knightly brother, for your patronage. We have recently discovered that the grand master will be in town next week; I must meet with him."

Joshua nodded nobly. "I will arrange it."

Merlin grinned and said, "As above, so below."

Feeling a bit understandably overwhelmed, Joshua rose, thanked them all, and stepped down off the camper and onto the street, almost getting hit by a passing car. He quickly stepped out of the way, brushed himself off, and headed back to work.

Chapter 11

Michelle looked closely at a map on her laptop. "On the way here, I noticed a nearby trailer park just outside of town." They reached the site just as the sun began to set over the lush green hillside. An hour later, Michelle began to skillfully prepare dinner. Merlin went outside to make a fire in the pit provided, and Frank decided to take a well-deserved nap before dinner. Michelle peered outside periodically to watch Merlin thinking, staring intensely into the fire. He then took a seat, picked up his guitar, and began playing as he grinned with delight. She saw Merlin in a different light and fell deeply in love right there. Accidentally burning herself on the stove, she let out a muffled scream, alerting Merlin and Frank to her side. Frank immediately went for the first-aid kit, while Merlin grabbed a sharp knife, cut the palm of his own hand, and touched her wound with it. A couple of seconds later, to her amazement and relief, her hand instantly felt fine. Still holding her hand, Merlin guided her under the sink faucet and ran cool water to wash his blood away. Their hands were perfectly undamaged. Frank watched, thinking, *Almost anyone else would call this the work of the devil.*

Merlin dried her hand with a nearby dish towel and gently kissed the magically healed area. All she could do was blush and thank him. After a good meal and a couple glasses of wine, Merlin and Michelle went outside for some fresh air and to enjoy the invitingly warm fire. Michelle began by saying, "Ironically, the word *renaissance* in French literally means 'rebirth.' What was it like for you back then?"

He tilted back his glass, slowly savoring the last gulp of wine, closed his eyes, and took a deep breath. "Endless battles churned out human carnage like meat grinders on blood-drenched fields across Europe, leaving death and disease in their wakes—and all in the name of supremacy for greedy, insecure kings."

With a curious expression, Michelle replied, "I don't understand—how could kings be insecure with all their wealth and armies?"

"Kings, my dear, sweet lady, had far more to fear, because they had much more to lose and did everything in their power to take what they could and keep what they had. Royal assassinations were ordered and carried out by other kings and sometimes within their own kingdoms. So the average life span of a king never lasted very long, thankfully. Warlords were their loyal watchdogs whose only legacy was promoting rape, torture, and senseless murder of all who opposed them, with a king's seal of approval."

He took a deep breath and let out a heavy sigh. "Having said all that, I would describe it mostly as terrifying, lonely, challenging, adventurous, enlightening, rewarding, and, through it all, magical."

Michelle fell back into her chair with a heavy sigh.

"The history books never determined if I was a myth, a magician, or a wild, hairy, forest-dwelling beast. I have also recently read that I may have even been an offspring of an incubus or the devil himself. Fortunately for me, the scribes closest to my time were lazy in the fact-finding department and possessed wild imaginations. What do you see?"

Michelle cupped his cheek in her hand, looked deeply into his eyes, and replied, "I see an exciting, warm, intelligent, talented, beautiful man."

He closed his eyes and said, "The end of one story always gives way to a new beginning of another." He picked up his guitar and resumed playing again as she rested her head on his shoulder. At that moment, time stood still for them both.

Fascinated and naturally inquisitive, she couldn't help but take out her notepad and pen. "Who were some of the most influential people in your life, in any order?"

Still quietly playing, Merlin stared into the crackling fire, and without missing a note, he replied, "To name a few, my blessed saintly mother, Alden; King Arthur; Ubach, a druid priest; Pope Urban II; Socrates; Leonardo da Vinci; Galileo; Buddha; and Shakespeare. Most recently, I've discovered an outstanding blues guitarist by the name of Stevie Ray Vaughan. Strange how some of the most impressive people always seem to die too soon, just like the brightest stars exploding in space. I truly believe that consciousness is inextinguishable and we are all, in effect, immortal." Merlin looked into the now-smoldering fire and said, "It's getting late, and we have a full day ahead tomorrow." Merlin put out the fire, and they both got ready for sleep.

Like clockwork, the sun climbed over the distant hills as the trailer park began to stir. Hovering over his bed, near the end of his meditation, Merlin touched down, feeling refreshed and ready for anything. At the same time, Frank prayed for guidance just outside their temporary home on wheels as Michelle showered and began to prepare breakfast. Minutes later, the distinct aroma of fresh coffee with bacon and eggs wafted over the campsite, prompting the men to wash up to eat.

Upon finishing, Michelle continued making notes on her laptop. She paused and gave her head a shake after finally coming to terms with Merlin's existence and accepting what it might mean to love a man like that. She thought to herself, *For someone with so much history, he sure manages to carry the excess baggage extremely well.*

Merlin moved up close to her from behind and smelled her freshly washed hair. Her heart began pounding uncontrollably out of her chest. Fortunately, she was able to compose herself and focus on the situation at hand for the sake of the mission before them, not to mention the ever-present priest. Ever aware of the feelings of those close to him, Merlin also played it close to his vest, like a well-seasoned cardsharp. As Michelle began another Internet session, she softly said, "When researching, you have to visit the most reputable sites—ones that are not mainstream media and hopefully have not yet been compromised. I have bookmarked these sites just for you."

Like a kid with a sweet tooth in a candy store, Merlin nodded and began searching with childlike wonderment, and soon he was surfing like a seasoned geek. Sometime later, Merlin did something he had not done since he was a boy: he blushed. "Wow, I'm rarely caught off guard, but this did it." He had accidentally stumbled on a pornography site, causing him to look on in disbelief.

Michelle looked at the computer screen and, innocently blushing herself, softly stuttered, "I forgot to mention those sites are freely available, mostly disgusting and, unfortunately, very popular."

Merlin grinned and replied, "Of that, I have no doubt."

Back on the road to London, now armed with a knight on the inside, Merlin suggested that they hope for the best and prepare for the worst. Along the way, Merlin took a short nap and dreamed of hundreds of ravens flocking wildly around the ancient Tower of London. A faint image of his saintly mother's face appeared and slowly became enveloped by the dense English fog as his attention turned toward the night sky. His gaze fell back down to earth and transported him to his favorite lake in France. He saw his once true love, the Lady of Shalott, taking one of her late-evening dips under a full moon. Her perfectly formed body gracefully glided in and over the silent black water, and then she dove under. Finally, she broke the surface, rising waist high above the waterline, exposing herself as only an earth goddess could, before diving down to the bottom again. Moments of dead calm passed; the surface appeared like a sheet of dark glass. A shiny steel tip and blade of a sword emerged from the stillness, reflecting the intense moonlight. Its majestically crafted hilt emerged from the bottom of the lake, exposing the unmistakable sight of Excalibur, the sword of justice, as she tossed it onto the soft, marshy ground at his feet. Shimmering water cascaded over her now-unrecognizable facial features. Slowly, as if happening one frame at a time, the water dissipated a trickle.

Much to Merlin's surprise, Michelle's face was exposed as she opened her blue eyes and pursed her lips as if blowing a kiss. Merlin woke still surprised but feeling refreshed and reassured, believing the visions must have been good omens. Now, with a good view of the Tower of London from a hilltop above the town, Merlin remembered one of the grandest castles in all of London. It had turned dark with evil, becoming a place of torture and imprisonment for the rebellious, the innocent, and the poor. Now, with all three of them looking at it, Merlin said, "It was considered at one time to be the center of hell, created by man and custom made for Satan." A tear welled up in his right eye and dropped down to the waiting palm of Michelle's hand. He quickly decided to lighten up the moment. "Wheresoever you go, go with all your heart."

Frank replied, "That's beautiful—is it yours?"

Merlin smirked. "Confucius—brilliant man." He tried to forget the horrific memories as he stared at the malevolent black spires that capped the haunted towers. Michelle received an e-mail from their newest member, Joshua, and read it aloud.

> M, the GM has agreed to meet with you and me for an hour at a safe location of your choice in London next Saturday at twelve o'clock sharp. He is scheduled to attend a meeting at two o'clock, followed by dinner here at the hall. As above, so below, J.

"Today is Wednesday; we have three days until then," Michelle added.

He shook his head from side to side and looked at the computer screen. "This form of communication is truly amazing. Please reply with the following: 'Thank you, J. The location will be in front of the Tower of London at twelve o'clock Saturday. Until then, M.' We must convince Grand Master Brother Trask of his fate and possibly countless others—which also means that I will be exposing my identity to him and perhaps even the world, and I was so hoping to avoid that." Merlin again took the lead. "Since we have the time, I would like to visit a place I once knew a few hours north of here. My dear friends, I value your lives as though they were an intricate extension of my own, so stay close and follow my lead, yes?"

Frank and Michelle were in complete compliance, and they headed north again, toward Scotland.

Chapter 12

Gabriel sat comfortably in his big office chair and made a call to his hardworking secretary, Joshua. "Have all the necessary arrangements been made for Brother Trask's long-awaited arrival?"

"Yes, Gabriel, everything is ready for this Saturday afternoon. The main meeting is set to begin at two o'clock sharp, concluding at four, followed by brandy and cigars in the main parlor room. A five-course gourmet dinner and an orchestra are all in line as requested, Brother."

"Splendid. Keep me informed! If anything goes wrong, I'm going to hold you solely responsible for it." Gabriel hung up abruptly in Joshua's ear.

Puzzled and concerned, Joshua was now even more convinced that Gabriel was experiencing a great deal of stress and was not himself. He also got the distinct impression that perhaps Gabriel was really planning to kill the grand master, as Merlin had implied.

Gabriel then made another call on his cell phone to his number one, Seth. "Do you have what is required for our VIP guest?" The anxious soon-to-be grand master paused to hear his response and then sighed. "Excellent. It is absolutely imperative that it look like an accident. If I am implicated or even suspected of being involved in any way, you alone will burn for it. Tell me you understand!"

"I understand completely, my lord, and I assure you that there's nothing to worry about. It will look like he died of natural causes. Trust me—it's what I do."

"Good, and while you're at it, I want you to keep an eye on Brother Joshua closely for a few days and report anything out of the ordinary! Seth, I do mean anything at all, yes?"

"As you wish, as always."

Gabriel concluded, "That stubborn old relic should have made way and stepped down years ago; his time is done." Two evil grins spontaneously stretched across their faces as Gabriel hung up. With a teasing voice, the pro grand master proudly looked at his reflection in a hand mirror he had pulled out from his desk drawer and said, "I, Sir Gabriel Hammond III, will soon fulfill my destiny as grand master. Then we and our new German friends will usher in a new world order no one will ever see coming." He pulled the mirror closer to his face, resting it on his cheek.

Later that morning, still irked over the unknown escaped prisoner, Seth accessed Interpol's mainframe for reports of anything unusual within the past twelve months. With keen, bloodhound-like senses, he looked for anything suspicious. Come midday, Seth received several hits on his latest obsession in search of the unknown prisoner. He carefully scanned the files and soon became interested in one particular report concerning an incident at the Roslin Institute, which was famous for producing Dolly the sheep. A group of concerned medical professionals had been suddenly relieved of their duties for a mandatory six-month period with pay and no explanation. Seth was a technology junkie and had always been intrigued with the cloning process; he was instantly hooked. Reading on, he learned that the head professor in charge at the time of the unexplained incident had recently retired and was conducting lectures at Oxford. The university's website provided the scheduled classes, and Seth noticed that there was one about to begin at noon. Since he had a little time to kill, he jumped into his new Jag, called his shadow patrol unit, and instructed them to be on full alert and stay close to the main hall until further notice. He arrived at the university and bought one of the professor's books in front of the lecture hall where the class was already in progress. The professor was in the midst of explaining the process of how relatively quick and easy it would be to clone a human being using some of the most advanced technology available.

Dr. Jack Bristol explained that the entire process, from a single cell to a fully grown human replica, was not only possible but had already been successfully executed; however, he did not divulge where, when, or by whom. "Unfortunately, I am compelled by personal and ethical reasons not to reveal the genius behind this most impressive procedure I ever witnessed. For some unknown reason, it's still against the law."

He winked and smirked. The young audience responded well to the professor, and another brief smirk appeared on his face, as if he were secretly feeding his own ego through this groundbreaking accomplishment. Seth noticed this and immediately felt even more intrigued as he leaned forward, sitting on the edge of his seat. The professor concluded, "Physically human in every way with only one question unanswered: Would he or she have normal levels of consciousness or be void of processing a simple thought or emotion? Our own personal experiences are absorbed and stored in memory cells at the base of our brains in the hippocampus and should generally, in theory, remain completely intact. Contrary to mainstream mind-set and available information in our ultra-modernized world, all is not as it appears. One might make the argument that playing God is a very dangerous game. I say science has naturally evolved and that we have simply progressed to the next level. It comes down to just one question really. If a loved one suddenly died and you could have them back just as they were in every way, would you welcome it?"

He received a standing ovation from the full class and clearly struggled to remain humble. Several students swiftly greeted him, asking the well-respected professor questions as he signed his latest book, fittingly titled *Rebirth*. Dr. Bristol seemed to enjoy rock-star status in the eyes of his adoring fans. Seth wondered to himself, *What if this seemingly vain professor successfully created a fully grown human clone? A six-month exodus of workers at the institute must have been exclusively for privacy, but could six months be enough time to be fully successful?* He now began to get the impression that the good professor had somehow managed it, had been sworn to secrecy, and was just dying to tell someone. Seth also got the sense that he might be on the trail to something extraordinary. He waited until the small crowd of groupies dissipated and then walked up to the professor to introduce himself. "I'm a great admirer of your work, Professor Bristol." He held out his hand for a shake and opened up his book for him to sign.

"You're very kind, Mr. ...?"

"Seth—just Seth. I was hoping that we could chat about your work over a frosty mug of Guinness at the pub across the way—my treat, of course."

The professor finished signing the book and jokingly replied, "You're not a government agent, are you?"

Seth replied with a chuckle, "No, sir. I assure you that government material, I am not."

"In that case, my good man, your offer is most humbly accepted."

"Splendid, my dear professor—splendid."

After the second round of pints, Seth ordered a couple of Grant's whisky shots, and then he inconspicuously dropped some powder into the professor's pint. Several minutes later, Seth smiled and politely excused himself and headed off to the men's room, where he pulled out his cell phone. He ordered his mobile control unit to meet him near his coordinates in thirty minutes, finished his business, washed his hands, and went back to tend to the professor. He returned to see the professor on the edge of unconsciousness, as if his head were filled with helium, floating without any neck support. Seth flashed an evil smile and poked the professor's head as if he were popping a balloon. He tried to resist bursting out with laughter as the doctor's head dropped; the professor blacked out the second the tip of Seth's finger touched his scalp. Seth helped the drug-induced doctor up and out of the pub and then drove the oblivious professor to a remote area and walked him up a ramp and into an unmarked black eighteen-wheeler. The back slowly drew up, closing behind them. A police cruiser passed the dark semi, shined a light at the license plate, and quickly moved away from the untouchable government-issued vehicle.

Seth gave the professor an injection to help his detainee regain consciousness. The professor soon woke, finding himself in a small dark room and bound tightly to a cold metal chair. Seth stood in front of him, holding a remote-control device in his hand. He hit the button for a second in an attempt to alert his guest to the level of seriousness he currently found himself in. "Doctor, I want you to know that I respect your work and accomplishments, but I am compelled to ask you some questions, and you, sir, will answer them to my complete satisfaction—or you will be very late for your next lecture. Does that resonate with you, Professor?"

Groggy, confused, and in panic mode, he began to whimper for his life. "Please, there is no need for this. I will tell you anything you want to know—just please stop this, for God's sake!"

"I find it interesting that a man of science would implement the word *God* in a sentence. You authorized and orchestrated a six-month mandatory, paid vacation for most of your staff and retired almost immediately at the end of that—why? What would compel you to do that unless you were conducting something illegal?"

Before the doctor could respond, Seth pushed the button for several seconds again, as if he were more interested in torture than an answer. Finally given a chance to speak, the doctor managed to utter, "I sent everyone away so I could work in private."

"Work on what, Professor? What were you working on that required that much privacy?"

"I cloned a human being."

"In your lecture, you said that it would require one year of close observation. How could the procedure be successfully completed in only six months?"

"He grew quicker than expected, but the body was the only thing that was developed; his brain was non-responsive."

Seth began to think about his escaped prisoner again and said, "Where is he now?"

"I don't know—I swear it!"

"What does he look like?" Seth yelled out.

The professor stuttered back in response. "Caucasian, six foot, about twenty-five, good physical condition, and long dark hair."

Realizing that this description fit his escaped prisoner, Seth could not resist placing his laptop close to the terrified captive's face. He played a copy of the surveillance video of the mystery man in the Masonic museum. "Is that him?"

The professor got excited and quickly responded, "Yes, yes, that's him." He took a breath to compose himself. "I mean, yes, sir, he was my patient—clone HC13. Is he all right?"

In an almost shocked state, Seth responded, "He is for now." Seth turned his back to the professor, holding the remote trigger tightly to his chest as he began salivating down the side of his mouth. The professor then volunteered information about the tracking device he kept in his vehicle's glove box. "Thank you, Professor. I've enjoyed our little chat. I'm going to release you now—from your life." He then gagged his victim, locked the remote button setting for twenty minutes on full, and exited the trailer, leaving the professor to die an excruciating death.

He rushed over to the professor's vehicle with one of his men, removed the tracking device, and reported back to Gabriel on his findings. Seth handed the professor's car keys to his man. "Put his body into this vehicle and roll it into the bottom of the river, and have the trailer cleaned and sanitized." Seth decided to get a good night's sleep and pick up the clone early the next morning to meet Gabriel as requested.

Chapter 13

That night, near the outskirts of southern Scotland, Frank, Michelle, and Merlin arrived at a site known as Caerlaverock Castle. "Are either of you familiar with this place?" Merlin asked.

Frank replied, "I have heard of it, but what's the attraction?"

"Here, my dearest friends, sat a haven surrounded by lush greenery and beautifully scented flowers, and once upon a time, I called this place home. I promised myself that if my memory was intact in the new world, I would come here to visit where this castle once stood so majestically."

Michelle reacted with a joyful bounce and shouted, "Let's have a picnic tomorrow."

The next morning was met with a clear blue sky and a warm, gentle breeze that carried the sweet scent of wildflowers through the camper. They all awakened refreshed, and the men washed up as Michelle prepared breakfast. Merlin entered the kitchen area, poured some coffee, and took a seat at the table. She inhaled the aroma of flowers wafting through the camper and sighed. "I understand your attraction to this place; it's beautiful."

"The two safest places I've ever known were the cave and this place. Extended periods of peaceful moments were rare and could only be found between battles. Two extreme opposites, but as deplorable as the mutilations were, the quiet times were equally as profound. We have a couple of days here, and I mean to relax, reflect, and study here. I have a lot to learn about this world, and it's the perfect opportunity to do so."

After a hearty breakfast, they all exited the vehicle to enjoy the day. Merlin took a walk down memory lane over the ruins as Frank prayed for the souls that had died protecting that sacred ground. Michelle couldn't resist collecting flowers, just as she had as a child, and made a flower band for her head and then continued writing in her journals. The morning faded into the early afternoon as Michelle went back into the camper, washed her hands, and began preparing lunch. She filled a basket with food, grabbed a bottle of wine and three glasses, and headed out to a nearby open area. Throwing out a large blanket on which to eat, she called the men to eat. With a glass half full in hand, Merlin offered a toast. "To new friends and peaceful moments."

After an enjoyable lunch, Frank pushed himself up to his feet. "I got something special from the pawnshop—now seems a suitable moment."

He went to the camper and returned with a long, narrow black shoulder bag.

"That's very attractive, my brother—does it come in red?" Michelle laughed.

He dropped the bag and removed a high-end spotting scope with a tripod. Frank set it up and focused over ten thousand feet away on a nearby river and motioned for Merlin to come take a look. As Merlin cautiously approached the unusual contraption, Frank and Michelle were all smiles, having a bit of fun. Immediately, Merlin was both shocked and intrigued by a mere gaze into a tube that could instantly bring everything afar to seemingly within arm's reach. Merlin paused in awe and shook his head at yet another impressive achievement in technology. "The lives we could have saved with a couple of these high up in the watchtowers—truly impressive."

Michelle said, "Not only a handy land scope by day but a powerful telescope at night—it's yours."

"You mean that I can see stars and planets up close? This is truly a magnificent device—thank you." With childlike wonder, Merlin continued scanning along the length of the river with his new toy. "Since I was a boy, I've always been mesmerized by objects in the sky, especially at night. Huh. I used to dream of bizarre alien creatures of various shapes and sizes with advanced interstellar capabilities, from primitive worlds like ours to older, ultra-advanced civilizations. Some were heartless world invaders with energy-extracting machines, others slaughtered civilizations for sport, and still others were more benevolent, life-loving, angelic beings who protected the weaker species. I've always wondered if they were simply conjured from a vivid child's imagination or actual images burned into my mind by the alien substance, or perhaps a bit of both."

Merlin later decided that he had been distracted long enough and should continue with his studies. After several hours of absorbing information at an almost superhuman pace, Merlin stopped to meditate. After a full day in this Eden-type setting, they capped the day off with a satisfying steak dinner. Frank soon decided to turn in early for the night. Merlin and Michelle grabbed a bottle of wine and a couple of glasses and scaled the ladder to the roof of the camper with his new toy to enjoy the starry evening show. They spent hours looking up into the night sky, enjoying each other's company, until Michelle finally fell asleep. He pulled her closer and cradled her body to keep her warm, closed his eyes, and took a few deep breaths.

JEFF BERG

A few seconds later, they both gently rose above the camper. After a slow, controlled descent to the ground, Merlin carried her inside, carefully put her into her bed, and warmly kissed her forehead. He so enjoyed the roof with his telescope that he decided to spend the rest of the night up there.

Wrapped in a blanket, Merlin woke up with the dawn and began meditating. An hour later, he opened his eyes, squinted, and focused his attention on a small, silent dark object in the sky, heading directly toward them. He quickly grabbed the scope and pointed it in that direction, and to his surprise, he saw a familiar black helicopter just over the clearing, moving quickly. Having the advantage of being in a mist and by a tree, Merlin looked down at the camper under him. "I've made all sorts of things appear and disappear but nothing ever quite so large before." With no time to alert his friends, he decided to spare them the trauma. With the helicopter almost upon them, he grabbed his large blanket and stretched it out at the perfect angle over the front of the camper, creating the illusion of invisibility. The helicopter hovered just above the tree line over the thin, misty vale for several seconds. A frustrated Seth gave the professor's tracking device a couple of whacks and tossed it into the backseat, believing it to be defective. He abruptly ordered the pilot back to the base, much to Merlin's delight and relief.

Frank and Michelle both woke up around the same time to the smell of fresh coffee Merlin had prepared. Merlin was sitting comfortably outside with mug in hand, feeling rather proud of his second escape from Seth. The others noticed that he slightly resembled the cat that had swallowed the canary. Michelle discreetly smiled and whispered to Merlin, "Thank you for last night. It was amazing, but I don't remember going to bed. How did I get there?"

Merlin fell into her deep blue eyes and answered softly, "I carried you down and put you into bed. Did you sleep well?"

A bit speechless, she replied, "Very well, thank you."

"It was entirely my pleasure, milady."

Frank, pretending to be reading, slightly shook his head and sipped his coffee, doing his best not to notice the obvious attraction between them. Not long after, they decided to pack up and slowly make their way back toward London. On the road again with Frank at the wheel, Merlin decided to relax and privately experience some musical videos for a while. He accessed his music library, extracted his eye screen, and inserted the spare earbud from inside the Bluetooth device for privacy and full stereo effect. Unleashing a full-on grin, he put on a pair of dark shades to cut out the glare and enjoyed the show.

Frank began listening to the local news, while Michelle, when not distracted by looking at Merlin, worked on her journals and diligently typed away. Suddenly, a news flash immediately caught Frank's attention: "The science world has suffered a great loss, as the body of distinguished Professor Jack Bristol was found early this morning. The coroner's official report stated that the doctor suffered a massive heart attack, lost control of his vehicle, and ended up in the Thames River. Dr. Bristol was lead scientist at the Roslin Institute, where Dolly the sheep was successfully cloned. He was lecturing at Oxford University and planning a European tour to help promote his latest book, *Reborn*. The professor is survived by his wife, three daughters, and four grandchildren. He will be missed."

Frank quickly pulled over to the shoulder abruptly, stopped, and exited the camper. The other two instantly realized there was a problem, and Merlin followed right behind his brother, who was already praying just outside the camper for the professor's soul and for his family. In a panicked state, Frank gave Merlin the bad news as they both took a seat on a large log lying at their feet. Frank gave his head a shake and looked over to Merlin. "If he truly died of a heart attack, then we need not worry, but if not, then that means that our evil friends can't be far behind, thus giving us good reason to worry—wouldn't you say?"

The only sounds were a cricket and the faint hum of a nearby power line. Quietly and cautiously, Michelle stepped out of the vehicle, quickly lost her smile as she looked at them both, and said with some apprehension, "What happened? Who died?"

Frank told her about the radio announcement as she took a spot on the log between them. Michelle turned to Merlin. "I don't want to alarm anyone, but what if Seth killed him and found the tracking device?"

Merlin reflected on the situation and responded, "There are more lives at risk here than the professor, the grand master, or us. We knew there would be certain unpleasantness during our little crusade." He stood up, looked at them both, and cleared his throat. "The death of the professor is sad and unfortunate but changes nothing. Our awareness has just been expanded, and that, my dearest friends, could work in our favor. We may be hunted, but we are anything but prey. We will meet the grand master tomorrow as planned." Merlin moved toward the camper, where he gestured for them to get back into the vehicle and then respectfully helped them both aboard to forge ahead on their journey. He felt much more confident to drive, much to the surprise and delight of his two friends. Merlin got comfortable, buckled up, checked the mirrors, and started the engine. He looked around for any oncoming traffic and smoothly rolled out like an old pro while his friends slowly began to relax.

Chapter 14

Back at the Masonic hall, Joshua worked diligently, putting the finishing touches on the annual event for their grand master, Brother Hayden Trask. Downstairs in the main kitchen, Brother Joshua had a word with the head chef about the extra-special dinner Saturday night. He stopped dead in his tracks when he spotted Seth going down a stairwell that led to the subbasement. Joshua squinted and cocked his head. "That man going downstairs—do you know where he's going?"

"He never said, and we don't ask."

The good knight cautiously followed the elusive Seth down the steps. When he got to the bottom, he peered around a corner and saw Seth pushing numbers on a keypad beside a solid steel door. The door opened, and Seth disappeared behind it. Now completely convinced that something was awry, Joshua turned slowly and headed back up to his office.

Inside the control room, Seth was immediately alerted to Joshua's presence outside the door by the live feed of a camera mounted outside, just above the door. He made a call to Gabriel and told him that Brother Joshua was beginning to suspect something and quickly becoming a liability. "I think he's beginning to suspect something. He followed me downstairs to the control room."

Gabriel frantically whispered back, "He knows nothing, so you are to do nothing; for now, just stay alert!"

"Yes, my lord." Seth hung up, releasing a low, primal growl. He then threw a nearby chair across the room in frustration, still irked by the escape artist.

Joshua arrived back at his desk, feeling like the only Mason, awakened to the nightmare. As a knight, he was compelled and obligated to do anything he could to right the ship. After a few minutes alone with his thoughts, he cleared his throat and headed toward the main boardroom for the pre-meeting before the event. Gabriel sat down with Seth in the main boardroom before anyone else arrived to briefly discuss the assassination of the grand master. Gabriel discreetly handed Seth a small vial of powdered barbiturates and a syringe filled with potassium chloride. "Empty this vial into his evening herbal tea that he religiously drinks every night before going to bed. We need to be sure that he won't wake up when you inject him; there's to be no sign of a struggle."

Seth smiled and tucked the items into his jacket pocket. Joshua arrived and caught a glimpse of them together, and he got a strange feeling in the pit of his stomach. The rest of their knightly brothers entered the room and took their seats at the large, round table. Gabriel stood to speak to his Masonic brothers.

"I want tomorrow to run like a Swiss clock, so all hands on deck, and be at the ready for anything!" He looked around at his knightly brothers, jerked his head back, and made a low but clear grunt to himself.

Unsure of Gabriel's odd gesture, the knights all looked at each other and then back to Gabriel and agreed. Gabriel glared at Seth briefly, and Seth returned a nod and a wink. On full alert, Joshua caught the short evil-to-evil exchange.

"We all have much to do before we leave today, so I'm not going to keep you here any longer than required."

For the first time, Joshua began to see Gabriel and Seth as they really were: bad men and not the honorable knights they'd pretended to be. Twenty minutes later, they adjourned to their respective offices and finished their business to prepare for the long-awaited event. Seth hung back to have a word with Gabriel.

"What are we to do about Brother Joshua? I fear that he's on to us both, and the damage he can do wouldn't take all that much effort."

Gabriel moved closer to Seth and whispered, "I believe you now, Brother; something must be done, and unfortunately, it must be tonight."

Minutes later, Gabriel quietly stood at Joshua's partially open office door. "How's it going, Brother?"

Startled and looking a bit nervous, Joshua kept his eyes on his computer. "Fine, Brother. Thanks for your concern, and you?"

Without an answer, Gabriel left as stealthily as he had appeared, leaving Joshua scratching his head. That evening, Joshua stayed late, putting the final touches on the preparations for the annual event the next night. He also sent an e-mail reminder to the grand master's secretary about his meeting the following day at noon with his friends. Almost fearing for his life but trying desperately not to look that way, he grabbed his keys and headed out to his car. Cautiously, he peered around each corner on his way, half expecting to find Seth waiting for him around every dimly lit corner. Looking out onto a mostly empty parking lot, he stepped into his car and began to feel much calmer. Joshua now believed without a doubt that if he had alerted his knightly brothers of the possible situation, their lives might also have been in jeopardy.

The second he shut the car door behind him, all the lights in the lot went out. Then two intensely bright lights from a large dark vehicle appeared from out of nowhere. Almost instantly, the vehicle plowed into the side of Joshua's car, knocking him unconscious. Everything went black. Gabriel watched from his ivory tower's office window, amused at the violent scene beneath his feet in the large parking lot surrounded by high stone walls with surveillance cameras perched on top of each corner.

Bleeding from his head and unconscious, Joshua was pulled out of his car and deposited directly into the back of the whisper-silent, dark tractor trailer.

The next thing he knew, someone was shaking his shoulder. Joshua opened his eyes and was immediately struck by a blinding light held directly toward his face. He quickly noticed he was bound to a metal chair inside a small, dark room. A small stream of blood trickled down the side of his head. Scared and helpless, he could only shut his eyes and pray. Although Seth was whispering to disguise his voice, Joshua recognized it immediately. "I know it's you, Brother. Is Gabriel here as well?"

Time ticked by, and in Joshua's traumatic condition, every second felt more like an hour to him.

"You're bleeding, my brother—that was a nasty accident. I personally didn't see anything; it was far too dark for anyone to see." As he moved toward Joshua, he released an evil growl. Eye to eye with Joshua, he said, "You are hereby charged with being a spy, and I am here to relieve you of your duties and what's left of your pathetic life."

"Please, wait—I've done nothing wrong!" Joshua cried out.

"That may be so, but we simply can't afford to take any chances—not now. Truth be told, Sir Joshua, I never liked you, and tonight I get the opportunity to express just how much." He was smiling from ear to ear, and his eyes opened wide with anticipation. He put a piece of duct tape over Joshua's mouth, set the remote control on full, set the timer for ten minutes, stuck out his tongue slightly to one side, and pressed the button. Joshua's muffled screams and wild jerks only seemed to excite Seth all the more. Before leaving, he turned to Joshua and said, "As above, so below."

He exited the trailer and instructed his driver, "Wait ten minutes, take his car to the river, put him inside, and drop it in! Only this time, make sure that it goes all the way down to the bottom!" The black-hearted knight smiled and breathed in the cool evening air, got in his car, and sped off. He then made a call to Gabriel to inform him of Joshua's unfortunate demise.

"Very well done, my brother. Now get some sleep; we have a big day tomorrow."

In full panic mode, Joshua looked up and uncharacteristically began praying to God. Just then, the power cut out, leaving him in a silent black void, and he accepted the real possibility that he had just died.

He caught his breath, held it, and heard a faint scuffle outside the room; then something heavy hit the wall in front of him. The ramp door behind Joshua slowly opened, and Frank and Michelle entered the pitch-black trailer with a flashlight. "Thank God you're still alive, my friend," Frank said as he began to separate Joshua from the chair. Michelle grabbed her scarf and poured some water on it for his head wound.

A dazed but elated Joshua asked, "How on earth did you know where I was?" He looked behind him at the gaping opening. "Where am I?"

Michelle explained, "You're in the back of Seth's private trailer—basically a torture chamber on wheels. We knew you might be in trouble, so we did a drive-by, saw this rig leaving the parking lot, and followed it here."

Shaking uncontrollably, with streaming tears of joy, Joshua said, "I owe you three everything. Thank you for my life—but where's Merlin?"

Frank responded, "He's taking care of one of Seth's men. We have to leave right now." They all scurried into the camper and waited for Merlin to arrive.

A couple minutes later, an out-of-breath Merlin arrived and said, "It does my heart good to see you alive, brave sir knight; you're a very lucky man."

"I have no doubt that I will never be able to thank you enough," said Joshua.

Frank looked outside toward the front of the truck's cab, asking, "Where's the driver?"

Merlin got behind the camper's wheel, started the vehicle, and replied, "Just behind the bushes; he's going to have a nasty headache when he wakes up tomorrow."

Frank gently put his hand around the back of Joshua's neck. "We're going to have you checked out medically; then, if all's well, you'll stay here with us tonight. Tomorrow is our big meeting; we need to stay focused and calm."

They took Joshua to a nearby clinic, where he was treated and released two hours later. They drove directly beyond the city limits and into the country, disappearing deep inside a trailer park filled with other campers. Morning broke over the nearby hilltops as Michelle exited the camper and looked up at Merlin, who was meditating weightlessly in a state of complete bliss. Not long after, the four crusaders sat around the table as Joshua told them everything he had been through and witnessed. With everyone now on the same page, Merlin decided to try to lighten up the moment by making things disappear and reappear and float—simple tricks he used to do regularly to keep children distracted for a while.

In the basement of the great hall, Seth called to check in with his mobile control unit. With no reply, he went back to the trailer, which was seemingly abandoned, still parked in the same spot. Seth went into the trailer and quickly exited, looking frantically around and inside the empty cab. He walked around back and found his man tied up. Seth quickly ripped the duct tape away from his mouth. With a loud, irate tone, Seth yelled, "What happened here, and where's the prisoner?"

"Sir, all I remember is the power going down and being knocked out."

Seth was reminded of the power going down before and immediately thought of HC13's escape, wondering whether there was a connection. He immediately called Gabriel to report on the situation. "No, sir, he escaped. When I came back, he was gone; my man was knocked out and tied up. He could not have done this on his own. I believe that illusive clone and his two friends helped him escape. I put the fear of God into him, and I wouldn't be surprised if he's already left the country."

"For your sake, Seth, you had better be right. It's too late to do anything about it now. I won't tolerate any more glitches, especially today! We must tighten up our security and see to it that nothing happens to alter our plan, or I will reach down your throat and pull out your little black heart myself!"

"Nothing more will happen, my lord. I swear it."

Chapter 15

Back in the underground control room, Seth sipped his coffee and ran through all incoming and outgoing e-mails. It wasn't long before he found three alarming letters from Joshua to someone he referred to as M. Wondering if that could possibly be the same M in the letter Gabriel had read aloud at the meeting, he quietly said to himself, "A private meeting in front of the Tower of London today at noon—we'll be there and ready."

Immediately, he informed Gabriel of this important piece of news. Gabriel said calmly, "I want you and your men to become invisible around the front of the towers before noon today and wait for them there." Gabriel paused to think for a second. "If you get a clean shot at that old relic Trask, Joshua, or the clone, take it! This could be the perfect opportunity to kill them all. If this meeting takes place, I will be most displeased."

Seth cleared his throat. "I fully understand, my lord."

Seth informed his team of the situation, and they positioned themselves discreetly around the front perimeter of the Tower of London and waited for instructions.

Later that morning, Merlin and company pulled into a spot by the towers as he reflected on how demonic this place once had been, sending chills down his spine. "It's imperative that we handle this most carefully. I fear there may be unfriendly eyes upon us, so keep out of sight and stay alert!"

Joshua said, "The grand master is a prompt individual, so we should have several minutes until he arrives." Joshua pulled a small object out of his pocket. "This tie clip is really a miniature infrared video camera that will record everything it sees. We can watch on this monitor in real time for his safety."

"How is he getting here?" Michelle astutely inquired.

"He doesn't drive, so probably by limousine."

Michelle began furiously typing her notes diligently. Everyone in the camper looked out in every direction for an approaching limo.

Seth and his men positioned themselves in and around the parking lot, not too far away from Merlin's new camper near the back.

The seconds slowly ticked away as all eyes looked feverishly for anything suspicious. Just then, a black stretch limousine with darkly tinted windows pulled up and parked near the front. Joshua drew a deep breath. "Okay, he's here—let's go!"

Merlin stopped him from exiting the camper at the last second and said, "Don't move," spotting a familiar black Hummer in the distance, under the shade of a tree. He scanned the area more intensely and spotted Seth waiting in his car on the other side. The new-world warlord looked out to certain areas, showing Merlin where his accomplices were positioned. Merlin mulled over the situation, looked at a map, and said, "They'll shoot us on site, so the plan has changed. I'm going alone." He looked directly at Michelle and said, "What we need is a quiet distraction of some sort."

Michelle smiled, stood, and excused herself from the room. She got up on the table and climbed through the ceiling skylight onto the roof. There she began to seductively dance and remove her clothing, catching most everyone's attention and causing quite a stir, creating exactly what Merlin needed. Cloaking himself from Seth's view, he exited the camper and quickly jumped into the backseat of the limousine, completely undetected.

The grand master and his driver were completely unfazed by Merlin's sudden appearance, as they were busy watching the beautiful woman dancing seductively on top of a nearby camper. After seeing Merlin disappear into the limo, she stopped dancing, blew kisses, and disappeared back down into the camper to an arousing chorus of car horns, catcalls, and the sound of a vehicle crashing into another. Even Merlin found himself off guard as he caught a glimpse of her exquisitely shaped body, causing him to briefly lose focus. "Sir Hayden Trask, I trust? Please excuse the bold intrusion, my lord!"

Alerted to Merlin's presence, the driver turned around just as Trask held up his hand and said, "I'm afraid you have me at a disadvantage, sir. Who are you, and why are you in my car?"

"My name is Merlin, but who I am is of no consequence. However, what I have to say is."

The grand master motioned for the driver to close the privacy window and replied, "Merlin—like the magician?"

Merlin smiled. "Yes, my lord—just like. Brother Joshua's life has been threatened, and he could not attend, but it was I who needed to speak with you personally. Your life and those of countless others are in danger, my lord. Your brothers Gabriel and Seth have been plotting to kill you and take complete control of the Masonic organization. They plan to start a war resulting in thousands of deaths, maybe more, and we cannot allow this to happen. This is true, my lord; I swear it."

Not looking excessively surprised, Trask raised an eyebrow, thought for a couple of seconds, and replied, "I've always suspected those two of being a bit odd, but assassination and war? I find that hard to believe even for them. I must hear this from Brother Joshua."

Merlin looked out to the camper and said, "He is just there—in that camper."

Trask responded, "You mean that one with the naked woman on top of it?"

Merlin tilted his head and nodded. "My humble apologies, sir; we required a diversion and were forced to improvise."

Trask cleared his throat. "No apologies are necessary, my boy; it was rather entertaining."

"Brother Seth and some of his minions are positioned around this area with guns trained on this vehicle. We have reason to believe they have already killed at least one man that we know of, and I'm guessing he was not the first. Call Joshua on your cell phone and tell him to look out the window for confirmation—would that suffice?" Merlin then pointed out Seth, who was sitting in his car and talking on his cell phone.

Trask made the call to Joshua. The GM shook his head, attempting to process it all. "Excuse me—I seem to be experiencing something of a surreal moment."

Merlin grinned. "Happens to me all the time."

Trask made the call and clearly saw his brother's face in the window as they had a brief chat, completely convincing him. "This is a real nightmare. What do I do?"

Merlin politely responded, "If I may, sir, I'm glad you asked. Attend the meeting as if you are totally unaware of what has happened here. Whatever you do, don't eat or drink anything that they offer you! They're more likely to try something later when you're alone and vulnerable, and we need to catch them in the act. Without any solid proof, we have nothing." He then handed Trask the small video tie clip. "Sir Joshua thought it might come in handy. Hidden inside is an infrared motion-detecting video camera that will record everything, day or night, in real time as a safety precaution."

Trask responded, "So I'm to be bait for my own attempted assassination then?"

"Unfortunately, that is the only way I'm aware of to catch them, my lord."

Trask took the device and put it on. "I have influential friends in law enforcement, and I will personally see to it that they get what they deserve and more." With a slightly nervous tone, Trask asked, "Will you and Joshua be close by?"

"Yes, we will be on the grounds; just call Joshua the moment you're alone in your room and wear the device, and we'll do the rest! It's imperative that you act as though nothing is wrong, and I promise you that we will expose them for the murderous warmongers they are."

Trask paused and then looked at Merlin and said, "My life is in your hands, and I'm not sure why, but I trust you completely. I want those two exposed and brought to justice and incarcerated for the rest of their miserable lives."

"Excellent. Now would you be so kind as to call Joshua back and tell him to wait a few minutes after we leave and then pick me up in front of St. Paul's Cathedral—if you wouldn't mind dropping me off on the way to the hall? They have not seen anyone enter this vehicle and therefore believe that this meeting never took place, giving them no reason to follow us."

"Not at all, Sir Merlin. I am truly impressed and forever in your debt. Sir Hayden then opened the privacy window and instructed his driver to go to St. Paul's Cathedral.

Seth watched them pull away, believing the meeting never took place, called off his men, informed Gabriel, and headed back to the hall. Merlin stood in front of the cathedral as the camper pulled up and stopped, and Merlin entered with a reassuring smile. "The meeting went well, and everything's set. It's time to replace this vehicle for something else more appropriate I have in mind." They all looked at each other curiously, and Merlin whispered to Michelle, "Thank you for that most unexpected diversion. It affected everyone within eyeshot, including myself in the process—well done!"

She gently grabbed his shoulders, got up on her tiptoes, and softly kissed his cheek. "You are most welcome."

Frank and Joshua looked on warmly. They slowly separated, and Merlin playfully looked her over and exhaled with a slight grunt, causing her to bite her lip and blush. "Let us depart to the nearest vehicle-rental facility, my good man!"

Minutes later, they found a luxury car rental company. They left the camper on the lot until their return and pulled out in a brand-new high-end black Mercedes with tinted windows and a content Merlin at the wheel. Now seated comfortably in the back beside Joshua, Frank asked, "What's our next move?"

Merlin looked at Frank's reflection in the rearview mirror. "We have several hours before our presence is required. We should stay out of sight until dark, at which time we are to go to the Masonic hall and wait some more."

Joshua joined the discussion. "In case you've forgotten, we're wanted men—to be silenced and disposed of like sacks of garbage."

With a renewed sense of self and a reassuring smile, Merlin replied, "It will be Trask and myself alone while you three safely watch on the monitor in a nearby hotel room."

Breathing a bit easier, they leaned back and enjoyed the ride. Michelle accessed the mapping system on the dashboard, looking for local accommodations. They decided on the Montcalm Hotel, where they soon arrived. Frank arranged for three rooms, again charged on the Vatican gold card. They went up to their rooms, where they unpacked and washed off the road dust. An hour later, they headed down to the restaurant for lunch and discussed how the evening could and should go.

Chapter 16

In the main boardroom of the Masonic hall, Grand Master Hayden Trask sat down for the meeting, with all the highest-ranking knights seated around the huge, round mahogany table. Trask's seat was in between Gabriel and Seth, which made him rather uncomfortable, but he managed to maintain his composure. Two long hours later, the meeting was adjourned, and the men all dispersed to their private offices. Gabriel escorted Trask to the VIP guest suite, pretentiously acting as though they were lifelong friends.

Seth got a call from his chopper pilot, who immediately informed him that the ground-positioning system device had been retrieved from the backseat of the aircraft. It had recently been checked out and showed activity with a moving target. His spirits quickly perked up, and he dashed up to the landing pad on the roof to see it for himself. Seth was surprised to find that the relocated target was only a few blocks away. He rushed back downstairs, climbed into his car, pulled a gun out from his glove box, and smoothly placed it in his jacket pocket. He then put on a pair of dark sunglasses and a ball cap and parked in the Montcalm Hotel lot. In the main hotel lobby, Seth sat and waited for his elusive clone to appear. Thirty minutes later, he was elated to see

Merlin and his two friends, along with Brother Joshua, and he let out a quiet "Jackpot." He stealthily followed them like a wild cat in tall grass, stalking his prey to the elevators. He watched the elevator's movement up to the fifth floor. Once on the same floor, Seth peered out of the elevator and saw Merlin chatting with Michelle for a couple of minutes; then each went into his or her separate room. With the hallway now clear, Seth moved along the wall toward Merlin's room and gingerly knocked on the door. Merlin opened the door, thinking that it was one of his friends.

The door burst wide open, surprising Merlin, and Seth entered and quickly closed the door behind him. He drew a gun with a silencer and said, "Did you really think you'd seen the last of me?"

"Not really. I knew we'd meet again—just not quite so soon. By the way, brilliant disguise." Merlin shook his head, adding, "You might want to consider a new hobby; torture just doesn't seem to be your forte."

A bit confused, Seth responded, "I'm here to finish from where we left off. This time, I promise it's going to be quick and painless."

Merlin curiously studied the weapon in Seth's hand.

"You do know what a gun is, do you not?" Seth said.

"Sure I do—it's a weapon designed for defense or used by pathetically impotent cowards such as yourself. And you didn't think I knew."

Seth gritted his teeth and turned red as a large vein in his head jutted out.

Merlin taunted him some more. "I bet you haven't slept a full night since we last met."

Holding all the cards, Seth quickly calmed down and grinned. "On the contrary, I sleep like a baby, especially after killing the prominent Professor Bristol." Seth cocked his head back and rolled his eyes. "It just occurred to me that he was your father of sorts, was he not, HC13? By the way, I'm also looking forward to finishing what I began with your friend Joshua as well."

Seth had hit a nerve; Merlin was now clearly upset. "Is it not customary to grant a dying man his last request?"

Seth paused and responded, "It's not my custom, but I will allow it—only because you still amuse me."

"How about letting me go?"

Seth laughed and teasingly said, "Ah, no—is that it?"

Merlin grinned. "I took a shot—pardon the pun! I was just wondering how and when you were planning to kill the grand master."

"Not exactly what I was expecting, but since you asked, by lethal injection in his sleep tonight."

Merlin nodded and took a deep breath.

Now just a few feet away, Seth aimed his gun directly at Merlin's chest and asked, "By the way, I would like to know—how did you escape my chair?"

Merlin replied, "Allow me to demonstrate!" A switch controlling the slightly open, thick drapes flipped them into the closed position. The room was now in complete darkness. Two muffled shots were instantly fired, followed by the sound of a body collapsing to the floor. The lights went on, revealing Merlin's lifeless body lying motionless on the floor, with two bullet holes in his chest. Seth promptly holstered his gun and exited the room, and the door quickly closed behind him.

Seconds later, a silent black void was interrupted by the faint sound of a heartbeat. Merlin's lungs re-inflated as blood began to pump throughout his body again, and the two holes closed as if they had never been there. Thanks to his ancient alien gift from the gods, Merlin was completely healed in minutes. A breeze from an open window wafted through the room, making the drapes open and close. He began to mentally see images of recent occurrences until the final flash of gunshots snapped him back into consciousness. After an hour of meditation; an extra long, hot shower; and a power nap, Merlin invited his friends into his room to discuss what he had experienced. "We have a new advantage: they now think I'm dead. They also believe that without me, Joshua is no longer a threat to them. That was one of the most singularly unpleasant experience of my lives, and I vow never to repeat anything like that again."

Michelle held Merlin's hand to comfort him.

"They're going to give Trask something to help him sleep, but he knows not to eat or drink anything they give him."

Joshua said, "There's a balcony in the VIP guest suite that overlooks the grounds on the top floor; you can gain access from the outside using a rope."

"I don't think I'll require a rope, but the second you see Seth walk into the room, call Trask's phone to alert us!"

Gabriel peered out his window and saw Seth pulling into the parking lot and waited for him in his office. "Where have you been, may I ask?"

Seth expanded his smile and responded, "Just taking care of some unfinished business, my lord—have I missed anything?"

Gabriel replied, "Not that I am aware of." He stared intensely at Seth. "Are we all set for tonight then?"

Seth cheerfully replied, "Yes, my lord—good to go, as they say."

"What have you done, Brother?" Gabriel asked suspiciously.

"Truly, Gabriel, I think you're being a bit paranoid."

Unamused with Seth's answer, Gabriel got eye to eye with Seth and said, "If I appear paranoid, it's because I have trust issues, and that keeps me one step ahead of everyone else. Can I still trust you, Brother?"

"I'm saddened that you even ask me that. Yes, my lord, of course you can!"

"We have an hour before dinner; I'm going to relax."

"Yes, my lord."

To pass the time, Gabriel went to his private office and polished his golden statue he kept locked in a closet in his office. Gabriel focused his gaze on the mirrored finish as he caressed and stroked it. "Soon I will be in complete control. I can almost taste supreme power."

Gabriel finally put his new priceless toy back in his closet and got ready for dinner. Live classical music played in the main dining area as hordes of well-dressed men and woman entered the huge dining room. Eventually, all were seated, and Gabriel formally introduced the guest of honor. The grand master, Brother Hayden Trask, entered alone in full dress and was escorted to the head table, where Gabriel, Seth, and a few other high-ranking Masons were seated. Dinner was served, but Trask unexpectedly refused to eat anything, saying that he had been battling the stomach flu and simply had no appetite. Gabriel responded, "That's a shame, my lord; we brought in one of the best chefs in all of London for tonight's service. By the way, how are things across the pond with our American brothers?"

"Strong and steadfast, Brother, as it should be." The grand master looked around. "Too bad Brother Joshua couldn't be here with us tonight. I so wanted to say hello and thank him for all his hard work."

Seth replied, "He's a good man. I'll thank him for you personally, my lord."

Trask looked into Seth's eyes and said, "Thank you, Brother."

Merlin and friends patiently watched and listened to everything the grand master's modified tie clip captured on their monitor from inside their hotel room. Just then, Brother Hayden excused himself and headed toward the main lobby. Gabriel moved close to Seth to privately say, "I have not been comfortable with the way things have been going so far, so I've set an alternate plan into action."

"I was not aware of an alternate plan."

"Consider yourself officially aware now! Brother Trask is a creature of habit—a shameful gambling habit. I gained access to his personal itinerary, and as it turns out, he's flying directly to Las Vegas from here before going home to Washington. He's staying at the Bellagio Hotel, and I want you to go there and finish the job! I have arranged for a high-class professional escort by the name of Sylvia to engage in conversation and vodka martinis with Trask the moment he arrives at his hotel, and she will spend the night in his room. She has the number to this temporary, untraceable cell phone and will contact you tomorrow around midnight their time. She will give you the room number and meet you by the door. In one hand, you will be holding an envelope containing five thousand dollars. You are to discreetly make an exchange for the keycard and finish this. I've given her a five-thousand-dollar advance for her services and promised another five thousand dollars when you two meet. He will be passed out from too much gambling, drinking, and extensive copulation—of that I was assured. Take his wallet and valuables—that should help make it easy for the local police to determine a motive. Hordes of tourists circulate every floor twenty-four-seven, so most anyone could have perpetrated the crime. I've even arranged to have the images of you going into the room and leaving it erased."

Seth chuckled with delight. "It's brilliant," he said just as Trask returned with a cup of hot peppermint tea he had prepared himself in the kitchen.

With the event winding down, Merlin went to the hall, cloaked himself in the shadows, and made his way past the guards. He then cleared his mind and levitated slowly up to the guest suite balcony. He reappeared after he climbed over the balcony. Sir Hayden arrived several minutes after. "How on earth did you get here without alerting the guards?"

"With respect, sir, all I can tell you right now is that you're safe. I will answer your questions later, but for now, please go on as if I am not here and try to get some sleep!"

Chapter 17

Several hours later, morning arrived, and there was still no sign of Seth. Still wearing the video tie clip, Merlin looked directly into the device and whispered, "Good morning, my friends. Please get some sleep now, and we'll meet up again in the restaurant in five hours!" He then respectfully woke up the grand master. "It would appear that they have changed their minds about killing you for now, but if I were you, I would initiate an investigation upon arriving back home! I have no doubt that your life is still in danger. What are your plans now, sir?" Merlin asked.

"I'm leaving in a couple of hours for the airport for a short stay in Las Vegas before heading home to Washington, DC."

"Then may I suggest that you increase your private security until this is all over? Gabriel must not be made grand master or all will be lost."

"The very minute I return home, I will look to build a case and have those two brought to trial. I hope I can count on you and your friends as key witnesses?"

"With a great deal of pleasure. Have a safe journey home, my lord!" Merlin walked onto the balcony, which was filled with early morning mist, and vanished. Hayden began to wonder if it had all been just a strange dream and went back to sleep.

Merlin took a twenty-minute walk back to his hotel room and took a short nap. Four hours later, Merlin received a wake-up call from the front desk and got ready for breakfast with his friends. Later that morning, they all met up in the hotel restaurant, as arranged. Merlin began by reassuring Joshua, "Seth and Gabriel are far too fixated on killing Trask to think about what to do with you right now. Trask told me that he will build a case against Gabriel and Seth and have them brought up on charges when he gets back home to Washington. We are all going to be key witnesses, and that will hopefully be the end of that, as they say. There is still the matter of the professor's tracking device still in their possession. I will most likely be found again—and soon—subsequently putting all of you in danger. We have two choices: either the device is obtained and destroyed, or the implanted chip is extracted from my body. Given the fact that I am immortal, the safer choice is clear."

Frank reluctantly responded, "We're going to need access to an operating room and, oh yeah, a surgeon."

Joshua smiled, adding, "As it happens, I know the chief physician at a nearby hospital, and he just happens to owe me a sizable favor."

Merlin returned the smile. "You have proven to be much more resourceful than I could have hoped for. I cannot afford to allow anyone else access to my secret; therefore, one of you will have to cut me open and remove the implant. Also, while we're at it, I would like the two bullets to be extracted as well if possible."

All three looked at each other, wondering who would be the one willing to step up and perform the operation. No words were spoken for a few seconds. They all took bites of their food, slowly chewed, and sipped their coffee. Finally, Frank spoke up. "I've had a little medical training, but I have never cut into anyone before. I've only ever sewn up cuts, and once I delivered a baby."

Merlin gulped down the last bit of coffee in his mug. "Excellent. Joshua, please make the call and arrange for complete privacy in one of their operating rooms as soon as possible today. Michelle, please source medical literature involving foreign-object extractions from the human body for Frank to study."

Michelle grinned at Frank. "Wow, it must suck to be you right now."

Frank shook his head and rolled his eyes in response.

Joshua made the call and said, "We have a room for two hours at three o'clock."

Michelle gave them both hugs and wished them luck. Merlin patted Frank on the shoulder and said, "I believe he is the one who will need the luck. All I'm going to do is simply lie down."

Now on a first-class flight to Las Vegas with his head literally in the clouds, Seth daydreamed of life in the new world, imagining himself and Gabriel at the top, with unlimited power at their disposal. The plane finally touched down at the Las Vegas airport. Ahead of schedule, he decided to kill a couple hours by touring the Strip, eating a fine meal, and maybe trying a little gambling and catching a show to pass the time. After having done all that, Seth got into character and put on his signature disguise: a baseball cap and dark glasses. He entered the Bellagio Hotel around ten o'clock. He received a call from the prostitute, Sylvia, who promptly told him to meet her outside room 512 in ten minutes with the cash. He casually finished his game with a slot machine and headed up to the room.

Just as Gabriel had said, hundreds of people were coming and going from every direction. As he got closer to the room, he spotted an elegantly dressed woman in a short dress and high heels standing by room 512, and their eyes locked onto each other. He then moved up close to her and discreetly handed her the envelope, and she handed him the keycard. He took the key but held tightly on to the cash and pulled her close against his body; his saliva streamed down the back of her neck. "Remember, we know where you live. Mention this to anyone and I will personally take great pleasure in shredding that beautiful face and body of yours into tiny pieces—do you understand?" He pressed her hard up against the wall, licked her neck, and released a carnal groan.

Speechless and shaking almost uncontrollably with fear, Sylvia could only nod in compliance. He released her, and she took the money and walked quickly into an elevator.

He took a deep breath, wiped his mouth, and then looked around calmly as he entered the room. He put on a pair of latex gloves and quietly crept toward the bedroom to find a content-looking Trask fast asleep in his bed. He grabbed the phone and hit Trask as hard as he could across his head; then he smothered him with his pillow to make sure he was dead. He found his wallet and valuables and turned over some furniture for effect. He then headed for the door and slowly opened it, removed the gloves, placed them back in his pocket, and headed for the elevators. Seth immediately went to the airport for the next available flight back to London.

Once Seth was home, Gabriel met him for a private celebration over a couple of cigars and a bottle of expensive brandy. Both completely elated, they toasted to themselves and their newly acquired power. "Las Vegas is an exciting town; I think I'm going to make it my annual vacation destination," said Seth.

The soon-to-be new grand master, Gabriel, hugged his number one and shook his hand. "Seth, my good man, you've just been bumped up to pro-master—congratulations."

Nearly speechless, all Seth could say was "As above, so below."

Finally realizing their long-awaited dream, almost in disbelief. Prone to pontification, Gabriel added, "I'll probably be getting a phone call anytime now, notifying me of the unexpected loss of our dearly departed grand master brother during a botched burglary. To which I shall respond with shock and great sadness, of course. Not long after that, there will be a fashionable, top-drawer funeral befitting a king, followed by a well-catered brunch. I imagine it will also include some good Scottish whiskey with fine cigars, and that will be the happiest moment of my entire life."

At a nearby hospital, in a private, sealed-off operating room, Doctor DeCarlo nervously scanned a step-by-step manual on how to retrieve a foreign object from the chest of a human victim. Merlin calmly got up on the table and lay down flat, and Frank administered the anesthetic as instructed. Frank strapped Merlin securely down to the table and looked over the surgical instruments as Merlin casually said, "Remember, I cannot die— good luck!"

Frank wiped a few beads of sweat from his forehead, took a deep breath, and carefully made his incision just between the ribs, roughly where the professor had told him the tracking device was placed. He inserted a fiber-optic camera into Merlin's chest, near his heart, and began frantically looking for the microchip and the two bullets. He soon found the chip and quickly extracted it. With about twenty minutes to spare, he was able to locate the bullets, which were lodged near each other, not far from Merlin's heart. Frank had to reopen the incisions several times, as Merlin's skin tissue kept closing up, which made it difficult to move the instruments freely. Frank completed the operation without leaving as much as a scar behind in under two hours.

Merlin soon woke up, and Frank announced, "The operation was a success. How do you feel?"

"I feel fine, but you don't look so good."

"That's because I think I'm about to faint." Frank collapsed just as Merlin grabbed him and got up off the table so that his friend could relax and recuperate.

"I've got you, brother; I've got you." He gave Frank a few moments and got him some water.

Back at the hotel lobby, the others greeted the two men with hugs and smiles all around. Michelle said, "You two must be completely exhausted!"

Frank and Merlin looked at each other and had a brief laugh together. Merlin responded, "We found time for a short nap, but we are a bit famished—anyone care to join us?"

They all happily headed into the hotel restaurant for a fine feast and eventually got a good night's sleep. The next morning, they met in the lobby for some tea and crumpets. Not long after that, Michelle opened her laptop, picked up her cup, and began reading the *London Times*. Suddenly, her teacup smashed to the floor, catching the attention of everyone in the restaurant. Looking a bit stunned all around, the group waited for her to finish reading. She quietly said, "He's dead!"

"Who's dead?" a startled Joshua replied.

Michelle lifted her head and looked around the table. "The Masonic grand master, Hayden Trask. It says here that he was killed last night in his hotel room while vacationing in Las Vegas, Nevada, at the Bellagio Hotel. The official police report says that an unknown assailant entered the room to steal cash and valuables while the victim slept. The report states that he was killed instantly by a blow to the head and smothered with a pillow. The Las Vegas hotel has been cleared of any negligence and regrets the incident, offering their utmost condolences to his family. He was one of the longest-reigning grand masters and was well respected by his fellow Masonic brothers. A private funeral will be held in his home town of Washington, DC, this Friday."

No one said a word for several seconds as the news began to sink in. Finally, Merlin shook his head. "This is too much of a coincidence. Gabriel must have had Seth follow Trask to this Vegas place and finish the job—I'll bet my life on it. Where is this Las Vegas, Nevada?"

Frank replied, "Across the ocean, in the western United States. I have never been there myself, but I have been told that it's sort of a large playground for adults in the middle of the Nevada desert."

Obviously shaken, Joshua cleared his throat and asked, "So now that he's gone, what do we do? I mean, Gabriel's won, has he not?"

Merlin replied slowly but firmly, "Gabriel has won nothing yet! Our only conceivable option now is to go to this Bellagio Hotel to try to discover exactly who the murderer was."

Michelle then said, "Someone in the hotel must have seen something or been caught on video. I'm with Merlin—we must try. If we can't implicate Gabriel or Seth in the assassination, then they will control our world, and I, for one, refuse to live under those conditions."

Frank then said, "God only knows what the pope's going to think when he gets the bill for our flights and accommodations to Las Vegas."

Merlin partially grinned and patted Frank on his back. "I'm sure he'll understand once we explain it to him."

Michelle perked up a bit. "I've always wanted to visit the United States." She looked directly at Merlin. "Your passport and birth certificate should be ready by now; I'll make the call."

Using the Vatican gold card, Frank and Joshua booked a trip for four to Las Vegas, and they all geared up for the flight later that night.

At the airport, they walked by some planes close up, and Merlin nervously swallowed. "I've seen these giant metallic airships in my dream visions; they seemed much smaller."

Sensing a bit of apprehension, Michelle responded, "Statistically, they say that it is safer to fly than to use any other mode of transportation."

Merlin cringed. "I'll bet that rumor was created by people in the flying industry to ease their customers' minds."

Merlin nervously presented his passport to the ticket agent, who carefully looked at the passport and then at Merlin. "Thank you. Have a good flight, Mr. DeCarlo!"

They entered the terminal and headed toward their plane, and everyone soon boarded and settled in for the long direct flight to Las Vegas, Nevada. Merlin found his seat beside Michelle, buckled up, and began to meditate until they were in the air and leveled out. Merlin ended up enjoying the flight, and he stayed awake the whole way, staring out the window in awe for the most part. He turned to Michelle and said, "In my other life, some believed that the world was flat and that nothing but hell lay beyond the edge—who knew? Plato said that ignorance is the root and stem of every evil. Once our mission is completed, I would like to see more of this amazing new world—join me?"

She looked at him as if he had asked for her hand and instantly said, "Sure."

He made use of this opportunity to access his internal computer for historical information and, of course, the music videos for breaks in between. Several hours passed, and they finally made a smooth landing at their destination. A bit disoriented and weak-kneed, they reached the Bellagio and immediately checked in. Merlin recommended that they all get some rest, freshen up, and grab a bite to eat before beginning their investigation. Later that day, they separated throughout the hotel to begin their search, armed only with questions and photos of Seth and Hayden. With nothing to show for their efforts hours later, they decided to break and regroup later that night. Merlin then said to Michelle, "On the way here from the airport, I saw a sign that said 'The Greatest Magic Show in the World,' and well, being me, I just can't resist the opportunity to see it. Would you care to accompany me?"

"I would love that—yes!"

Chapter 18

Merlin was dazzled by the elaborate display and special effects of the show. Afterward, Merlin was so deeply impressed with the magical experience that they waited for the magician at the elevators to thank him personally for the exhilarating experience. When the famous illusionist approached, Merlin briefly expressed his gratitude and was delighted to find the new-world legend humble and cordial. Just before the magician went up in the elevator with a small entourage, he told Merlin, "I have the strangest feeling that we have met before."

"Oh, I doubt that, but I am very pleased that we have now."

They shared a smile and shook hands, and the illusionist invited Merlin and Michelle back to another show anytime as his guests. They both happily agreed and headed back to their hotel.

Merlin and company met at one of the cafés at the hotel for a quick bite before their next move. Joshua said with a certain degree of excitement, "I just spoke to my American counterpart, the grand secretary to the United States. We correspond on a regular basis, and I consider him a trusted friend. I have arranged for us to have a private chat with the head of security at this hotel in twenty minutes. I have been assured of their full cooperation."

They were soon escorted into the security room for a private viewing of all the hotel's video footage from inside and outside the hotel on the night of the murder. Merlin reminded them, "Remember to look for anything unusual; stay focused, and remain patient!"

After over three hours of intense viewing, Merlin spotted a suspicious-looking man in the lobby, slightly resembling Seth, wearing a cap and a pair of dark sunglasses. An expression of relief appeared on Merlin's face as he moved closer to the monitor, saying, "There you are!" They all crowded around the screen and watched a man who could well have been Seth wearing street clothes and a cheap disguise.

Michelle pointed out, "That certainly looks like him, but that's all we know."

Merlin confidently stated, "It is him all right; he wore exactly that when he shot me."

As they continued staring at the scene, they saw Seth answer his cell phone and, without saying a word, hang up and head straight for the elevators. They patiently continued watching as the elevator stopped on the third, fifth, ninth, and fourteenth floors and then went back down again. Merlin then looked at the head of security and politely asked, "What suite did the murder victim stay in?"

He checked on his computer. "Mr. Trask stayed in suite 512."

Via footage from a video camera inside the elevator, they clearly saw Seth exit on the fifth floor, as expected. "Are there also cameras on the floors?"

"Yes, there are," the security officer replied.

Immediately after that, the picture went blank for about thirty minutes on the fifth floor. The hotel manager raised an eyebrow and said, "Huh, that's a first. After the murder, the police took over this room to conduct their investigation. No one else had access but them."

Joshua harshly whispered, "Gabriel."

The security guard leaned forward toward the screen and said, "Without video of someone going in or coming out of the room, there is no evidence."

Everyone but Merlin believed this was now just another dead end. He said, "Okay, can you begin the video from the time Trask checked in to the hotel?"

"Sure, we can do that."

They soon saw Trask entering the hotel, checking in at the front desk, and heading straight to his room. They fast-forwarded to when he came back to the main lobby and into the casino, where he was unexpectedly approached by a sultry woman in a revealing black dress and high heels. They spent hours together, had dinner at the Bellagio's famous steakhouse, and then went up to his room for approximately three hours.

Merlin watched the last few segments again and said, "Have you seen this woman before?"

"No, I'd remember seeing her, but she might just be new in town. I mean, a beautiful woman alone in Las Vegas is generally looking for one thing, and it is not our world-famous porterhouse."

"We must find this woman!"

The officer suggested, "I would try local websites; you may get lucky. No pun intended."

Joshua then requested a photo of the mystery woman and thanked the guard for his help. They exited the security room and headed back up to their rooms for a good night's sleep; they would begin their search for the mystery woman in the morning.

Early the next day, Michelle volunteered to take charge and coordinated the search by compiling a list of addresses of thirty of the most expensive escort businesses in the Las Vegas area, ranging from the farthest away to the closest. "Okay, I'm splitting this list into four even sections. I've made copies of this woman's face—someone's bound to recognize her. The number of our hotel front desk is at the top of each list. Call in every hour for messages whether you find her or not. Are there any questions?"

Appearing quite impressed, the three men could only shake their heads and smile.

"Okay then, good luck!"

They climbed into four cabs and set off in different directions. Five long hours into the search, Frank finally learned that their mystery woman's name was Sylvia, and he called the Bellagio to leave the message. They soon regrouped back at the hotel and sat down at one of the restaurants for a snack and a chat. Merlin decided to set up a kind of sting operation whereby he would have her come to his room so that he could question her alone. After dinner, he called the escort company, which immediately arranged for Sylvia to be at the hotel within the hour, almost as if he were ordering an expensive pizza.

She promptly arrived, and Merlin greeted her and invited her in and immediately delivered his true intention. In his last life, one of Merlin's many hidden talents had been getting people to tell him things most would never say to anyone else. He began, "A couple days ago, a good friend of mine was killed here, and I know you're involved somehow indirectly."

"I don't know what you're talking about! I'm out of here!"

"Please, you were with him the night he died, and that makes you a key witness."

Sylvia abruptly got up and ran toward the door to leave, but he had quietly wedged a piece of wood under the door, anticipating an anxious getaway. "Look," she said, "all I know is that someone paid me a lot of money to show someone a good time and afterward hand the key to some guy who said that he would kill me if I told anyone. I've met all types of men, so believe me when I say that this guy meant what he said. For all I know, you're working for him to do just that."

"My dear girl, he happens to be my nemesis. I and my friends are working hard to see him brought to justice. We have traveled a long way to see to it. Besides, if I were here to kill you, we would not be having this conversation."

Merlin put Sylvia's mind at ease, and she took a deep breath and said, "I wish that I had never taken that money; I've been fearing for my life ever since. That kind man was killed because of me—what have I done?" She sat on the edge of the bed, dropped her head into her hands, and began to cry.

Merlin reassured her by saying, "From my point of view, all you're guilty of is having bad judgment."

As though a huge weight had been lifted from her shoulders, she hugged Merlin, calling him her savior and offering to pay back the blood money she had accepted.

"I have a better idea—I want you to testify as a key witness in his trial that will put him away for life, but you would have to come to London to do it. Will you?"

She complied, showing him her driver's license and handing him her personal phone number. "Call me anytime, and I'll be on the first flight to London—I swear it!"

Merlin thanked Sylvia and gathered his team to announce that they had what they'd come for and that it was time to go home.

Chapter 19

Gabriel got a phone call from the secretary of the American Masonic order in Washington, DC. "It is with great sadness that I officially inform you of the sudden passing of Brother Grand Master Prince Hayden Trask." With growing impatience, Gabriel waited for the secretary to stop talking. "He was murdered in his sleep for money. I am confident that you will carry out your new position admirably with grace and honor, my lord."

Gabriel finally replied, "I don't know what to say; I'm in shock. Have they found the killer?"

"Not yet, but they assured me that they will do everything in their power to apprehend and punish the one or ones responsible."

Gabriel concluded his flawless performance with "As above, so below."

He worked on Trask's eulogy in front of a full-length mirror, trying to contain his elation, with little success. Just behind him in the reflective background sat his priceless golden dragon, which exceeded his wildest dreams exponentially—the icing on the proverbial cake, as it were. Smartly, on a trolley, he rolled the brilliant statue back into his hidden wall closet. He carefully selected one of his best suits and symbolic accessories for the full-dress effect, right down to his lucky silk boxer shorts. The newly appointed pro grand master, Seth, along with all the highest-ranking UK knights packed their overnight bags for the long trip across the pond to Washington.

As the knights all boarded the plane for the United States, Merlin and company were already in flight, heading for home. Merlin was staring out the window, mesmerized again in the giant metal airship, burning every image into his mind to remember for future inspiration. He eventually nodded off and vividly dreamed of flying alone through the clouds, but not with the aid of a plane. Now in total control, gracefully gliding about, he saw an approaching airship that slowed down and came within inches of him. Flames ignited like a bomb exploding, quickly spreading through the entire plane. He saw Gabriel and Seth in one of the windows, laughing insanely at it all, as if Satan and the Antichrist were sharing a Coke and a smile.

The airship moved away at normal speed and exploded into a million bits, snapping Merlin awake.

Instantly alerted, Michelle asked, "Did you have another vision, or perhaps it was just another bad dream?"

"I'm inclined to believe it was a bit of both. I believe that Gabriel, Seth, and their knights are en route to Washington to attend Trask's funeral—which gives us the window of opportunity we require to continue on our treasure quest. I also hope to find something to connect them to the grand master's murder—something incontestable. We will still have to get past their security. We'll regroup with a new plan back at the hotel."

At Washington Memorial Funeral Home, a long line of black stretch limousines pulled over to the side of the cemetery road. Several hundred of the highest-ranking knights across the globe, in full formal dress, slowly made their way to the burial site of

Prince Hayden Trask. Gabriel and his knights were among the first to arrive at the gravesite. One of three other Freemasons who was already there greeted Gabriel. "He was the perfect knight of the highest order."

All Gabriel said was "Yes, he was that."

With his true feelings hidden behind a dark pair of Gucci's, Gabriel enjoyed the moment, looking around at the large grieving group of people focused on the casket. He turned to whisper something to Seth. "He was an old stiff when he was alive; now he's an old dead stiff. I think I like him much better this way."

They both shared an evil chuckle just as Gabriel's name was called to say a few words for the dearly departed. He straightened his tie and lightly cleared his throat. "I've known Hayden for many years; he was my boss, my mentor, and my good friend." He quickly motioned as though he were wiping a tear from beneath his expensive shades. Several curious looks came from some of the English knights as their new grand master continued. "It's been an honor and a privilege to serve such a passionate man and a great leader. His wisdom will always be remembered and his dedication respected. Farewell, old friend." As he sighed, he looked down at the casket and shook his head as if in complete disbelief. Again he motioned to wipe away another tear as if it were just about to hit his cheek. He capped the speech off with "As above, so below." He then extended his sincerest condolences to Trask's family, and Scottish pipes played "Amazing Grace" as the casket was slowly lowered into the ground. After several minutes, people began to disperse to their cars for the wake a few miles away in the main Washington Masonic hall.

At the Dorchester Hotel in London, Merlin's team met in the restaurant to formulate how they were going to infiltrate the

Masonic fortress and what to look for once inside. Joshua presented a computer file blueprint on the building's layout and offered insight on the internal and external security systems in place. "It's standard practice to reinforce the security patrolling outside when the head people are absent; no one is allowed anywhere near the hall. I think that our best chance is to pretend to be the night custodians. The cleaning crew enters through the underground parking in a company vehicle every night at eight o'clock sharp, working through the night. We could pose as them, giving us access to almost any room in the entire structure."

Merlin said, "It's the restricted areas that interest me—where are they?"

"Seth's and Gabriel's offices, of course, and the main control room in the subbasement, but those are all locked up tight. Internal and external motion detectors are always active, and video surveillance cameras are always on around the entire building. We can expect approximately six security guards inside and Seth's shadow patrol unit just outside."

Merlin nodded and said, "Good. Then if there's nothing else, this is how it's going to go. If you have any doubts, please speak now; we are among friends here."

Eight pairs of eyes looked at each other in silence as they patiently waited for Merlin to continue.

In response, he drew a deep breath. "Thank you all for your dedication and friendship; it warms my heart in a way that words cannot express. We have a few hours until the cleaning staff arrive, so let's go over the plan carefully together. Joshua, who was the person normally in charge of arranging for the cleaners in the past?"

Joshua smiled. "As luck would have it, that duty fell upon me."

"Perfect. Call them and tell them to meet us a block away from the hall, where we will pay them triple their regular rate in cash. We're going to need full use of their vehicle, equipment, and uniforms for the night. We will meet them back at the same spot approximately six hours from the time we take the truck."

Slowly nodding as the wheels spun, Merlin continued. "When we arrive at the hall, don't make eye contact with anyone! Joshua is familiar with the routine and nuances, so remember to follow his lead. No one do anything to raise suspicion, and we just might make it through the night with all of our wobbly bits intact. Once we are upstairs and reach the offices, Joshua will point out Gabriel's lair, and I alone will enter and access his computer."

Michelle chimed in to say, "Take this flash drive, and download anything you think might be incriminating or questionable." She showed him how it was done. "The only problem is that without Gabriel's password, we're sunk."

Merlin confidently nodded again and grinned. "Leave that to me—we're ready."

Chapter 20

Three hours later, Joshua pulled up in a clean, fully loaded white cargo van with everything from equipment to uniforms. They all climbed in and got into character. Merlin turned to Joshua, jokingly asking, "You aren't, by any chance, chummy with any of the night-time security guards, are you?" He tried hard not to allow the others to notice his slight concern for not knowing Gabriel's password.

The rendezvous was executed right on time without a hitch, and they all put on the crew's white overalls and signature baseball caps. They soon successfully entered the building unmolested, and within an hour, they made their way up to the next level. With heads down and silent, they made their way through the majestic halls and up the freight elevator with a large floor cleaner in tow and supplies neatly on a trolley. Without a word, Joshua pointed straight to Gabriel's office at the end of the hallway, as instructed. He then tapped Merlin on his shoulder, waited for him to turn his head, and raised his eyes upward. An active video camera overhead was trained directly on Gabriel's office door. Merlin winked at Joshua and whispered, "I'm going to find a back door—spread out and be careful."

Wearing the expression of someone who had just unexpectedly sat in a big bowl of goo, Joshua continued his search. Merlin waited for them to disappear into another office and then walked down an opposite hallway until he came to a large window that was slightly ajar. Looking outside, he spotted two guards on patrol and waited for his moment. Seconds later, Merlin made his move, quickly stepping up and out onto the narrow ledge. He calmed his mind, closed his eyes, and slowly floated up just enough to firmly plant one knee and both hands on the rooftop. Staying low, he soon noticed a strange white circle pattern painted on the roof, with a large letter G in its center. Merlin quickly realized it was a landing area for their silent, wingless air machine. He moved straight across toward Gabriel's office window, but instead, he found a handle with a latch that opened a small trapdoor situated just past the edge of the painted circle. It opened wide up with ease, and he quickly lowered himself down, using a conveniently built-in ladder. Once firmly on the floor, he looked around, took a seat at Gabriel's desk, and booted up the computer. Merlin closed his eyes, cleared his mind, and began breathing deeply. On the third breath, he opened his eyes and began by typing all the most obvious words first. He picked up an envelope and tried the address.

He looked around the room at paintings and photos and then quickly zeroed in on a bronze bust with a gold plaque that read "Adolf Hitler," giving him pause as he recalled reading about what this madman had done. "Hmm." He hummed curiously with a sideways grin, typed in the word *Hitler*, and instantly gained access, exposing a Nazi symbol on the desktop. He then plugged his flash drive in and downloaded everything and anything they could use.

He quickly began to click and drag files, folders, and e-mails into the device as instructed, including a document with a title written in German. Easily accessing Gabriel's e-mail, he grabbed everything and anything he could and then quickly disconnected and powered down the computer. Ahead of schedule, Merlin began looking around, confident that the dragon would either be there or at Gabriel's home. It didn't take long for Merlin to notice the poorly hidden compartment inside Gabriel's personal closet that contained his long-lost statue. A tear instantly came to his eye. He pulled out a rope and a blanket from inside his uniform and securely tied the blanket over the heavy object. He climbed the ladder, sat down, and braced himself for the lift. With every ounce of strength he had—and a few he didn't know he had—he hoisted the object all the way up safely to the rooftop and closed the hatch. At the far edge of the roof, he anchored one end of the rope, looked around for any guards, and carefully lowered it down to the side of the open window. He then safely found the window ledge, quickly grabbed the dangling statue, and pulled it inside.

Spotting the rest of his crew, he retrieved the cleaning cart they had brought up and placed the statue carefully inside without his friends noticing. He then closed the window, caught his breath, and let them know it was time to leave. Merlin rolled the cart right into the truck using a loading-dock ramp, and they managed to leave as easily as they had entered.

Merlin turned to Joshua at the wheel. "Drop the three of us off at our car first! We will pick you up straight away at the corner."

"What do we have now that we did not have before?" Michelle sweetly inquired.

"I'm sure you remember meeting Seth in the forest by the waterfall. An object was removed from the cave and placed into the helicopter." The van stopped just as Merlin jumped out of the back and asked Frank for his help. He then uncovered the statue that snugly rested inside their trunk as his friends gasped in awe. "This is mine. I made it and sealed it in the cave, knowing that it would make a perfect distraction from the real treasure—me!" he explained with a humble look and a laugh. "I mean, it made perfect sense at the time! It was poorly hidden in Gabriel's office wall, so naturally, I'm reclaiming it."

After a good night's sleep, Merlin and his friends met in his room to go through the cache of files and letters to and from Gabriel. They picked up Joshua and then drove directly to a pawnshop so that Frank could get two slightly used laptops. Upon Frank's return, Michelle smartly downloaded copies from the flash drive for the guys. Unable to contain their curiosity, Joshua, Frank, and Michelle all began the search right there and then in the car.

After a couple hours of intensive reading with no luck, Joshua gasped. "Oh my! Here's a letter from the secretary of the leader of the Nazi party, dated three days ago: 'The transfer of funds has been received, and we are now set to put our plan into action. We now have key people in Europe's water, food, and pharmaceutical distribution centers in position, waiting for your signal to begin as instructed. Heil Hitler!' Merlin, I'm no expert in your laws yet, but I'm inclined to believe that is significant evidence, is it not?"

Confidently speaking for the others, Michelle said, "Yes, I'd say that's all the proof we need right there, including a copy of the hotel video, Madame Sylvia, and ourselves—absolutely."

Frank chimed in. "Okay, now that we have all this evidence, what do we do with it? I mean, for all we know, Gabriel has half of Scotland Yard in his pocket, along with most of the local bobbies, not to mention a handful of judges!"

They all looked over at Joshua, who shrugged and nodded. "I wouldn't be at all surprised. I've often suspected, but that's never been discussed in my presence. Frank may be quite right."

An unusual amount of time passed without a word. Finally, Merlin said, "There is only one person who can help us all." Looking directly at Frank, he added, "We're going to put our trust in the Lord!" He grinned.

They all nodded and smiled back in compliance. Frank replied, "I'll deliver the message to His Holiness, but what makes you believe that he would be willing to get involved with all this?"

"With faith, Brother—with faith!"

Frank performed his now-signature move: looking up, clutching his crucifix, and shaking his head as if to say, "God, please forgive us." But instead, he said, "I'll arrange for the tickets."

Back up in the air, Merlin looked out the window in awe. Through most of his life, he had dreamed of traveling vast distances in just a few short hours—the chance to live in peace and see the world. A couple of hours later, they landed at the Fiumicino Airport in Rome and took a taxi to Vatican City. As they pulled up to the basilica, Merlin started remembering the last time he had been there, several centuries ago, performing for Pope Urban. Frank found a priest by the main front entrance, and within a few minutes, they were being escorted to the pope's office. When they reached the door, their escort told them to wait a few moments for His Eminence to arrive. Seconds later, the pope quickly turned a corner and greeted Frank with a smile and a hug, completely surprising everyone, especially Frank.

"Your Eminence, these are my friends Joshua, Michelle, and Merlin."

Seeming somewhat amused, the pope moved his head forward to Merlin, asking, "Like the magician?"

Merlin smiled and took a knee. "At your service, my lord."

They each addressed His Holiness in the proper fashion.

"Your friends are my friends, my son. It's good to meet you all; please come in, and we'll have some tea!"

They all took a seat as the pope asked Frank, "So has your mission been accomplished?"

"Not quite yet, Your Holiness, but perhaps with your help, it might be."

"When I first read the letter from my ancient sainted brother Urban, it was a defining moment in my life. I have done and will continue to do anything in my power to see his request through, whatever the cost." Now wide eyed and on the edge of his seat, he leaned forward and said, "How can I help?"

Frank and company told the story of what had happened until the present moment, excluding the whole cloning thing, being it was anti-Catholic and all. The pope listened carefully for twenty minutes, and when they were finished, he stood up and went over to the window for a pause and a breath of fresh air.

"Please give me a moment, my friends; that's quite a bit to process." Sipping his tea, he found his seat again. "I'm sorry for your loss. I remember meeting Sir Hayden Trask once; he was a good man."

They all looked at each other, and Frank knelt. "Forgive me, Your Eminence. I was presumptuous and thoughtless, but we had no other option and would never assume."

The pope stopped Frank right there, touching his head and helping him to his feet. "There is no need for explanation, my son; I understand your position completely. It also explains the trip to Las Vegas and a few other oddities." He released a hearty chuckle. "I have the ear of a very influential friend who holds an influential seat in the European Union; he will help us. I will make a call to him immediately; please wait here and finish your tea."

Fifteen minutes later, the pope returned. "I've spoken with my friend, and he said that he will look into the situation personally and let us know what his findings are. He asked for three days to assess the situation and come up with a proportionate response. In the meantime, I insist that you stay here at the Vatican as my guests until this is resolved! At least until the smoke clears up enough for us to see a bit better, yes?"

Merlin looked around the room at his friends' relieved faces. "We would be most honored to stay as your guests, my lord; thank you for everything you've done."

Seeming a bit conflicted, the pope said, "I'm not sure why, but I have the distinct feeling that it is I who should be thanking you, Merlin. Are you, by any chance, a religious man?"

"Only in spirit, my lord."

"What you are is something of an enigma, and I would love to know more about you—perhaps tonight in the courtyard for tea? Father Fantorio will escort you to your rooms; please make yourselves at home, and if there is anything you require, please just ask—anything at all!"

After settling in their rooms, they met out by the beautifully arranged courtyard. "He sure seems interested in you—why do you think that is?" Michelle asked Merlin.

"I'm not sure, but after all he's doing for us, I think he should know the whole story."

Frank interjected. "You do understand that cloning has been declared an unholy act by the Church?"

Merlin replied, "I understand, but he still has the right to know. He is an understanding, well-educated man. I doubt he'll burn us at the stake."

The sun began to set, dimming the entire courtyard as the pope approached the crusaders for another chat. Hours passed as Merlin eloquently told his life story from the beginning to present day, from his blessed mother to the fallen alien star to his deal with Pope Urban II and his prophecy into this world. By the time he was done, the pope was understandably in complete awe. With a high level of apprehension, he finally replied, "I can't decide whether I should have you removed from here immediately or embrace your uniqueness. I have never been so conflicted in my entire life. I'm going to pray for you all and give this much thought tonight, and I'll give you my decision in the morning."

"I understand, my lord, and we will, of course, respect it."

The next morning, Father Fantorio softly knocked on Merlin's door. With a stern but humble voice, the priest said, "Mister Merlin, His Eminence requests your presence in his office within the hour!"

Just finished packing his bag, he opened the door and replied, "Yes, thank you, Father. I'll be right there."

Appearing exhausted but resolved in his office, His Holiness answered the door, allowed Merlin to enter, and kindly asked him to take a seat. "I've been up all night grappling with your incredible story. Unfortunately, there is nothing in the scriptures that covers any scenarios quite like this; this sets a new precedent. Our belief is that your kind is—if you'll excuse the interpretation—an abomination derived from evil. But you are obviously not an evil man, thereby presenting something of a dilemma." He looked at Merlin carefully, slowly shaking his head. "This goes against everything I stand for, but again, there's always an exception to the rule, is there not?"

"I believe that to be true, Your Eminence." They shared a short a laugh together to break the tension.

"Whether or not you are of natural origin does not outweigh the facts of the dire situation you and your team have apparently uncovered. The only moment in existence is the present; the past is irrelevant and the future unknown. It is our actions that define us, and yours appear to have the best of intentions."

His Holiness extended his arms outward for a hug, personally welcoming Merlin into the new world. "Now, if you'll indulge me, my son, there have been quite a few technological upgrades to our library since your last visit, and I invite you on a tour."

"You remind me of Urban, my lord; he too was thoughtful, intelligent, and generous. I remember him saying that good leaders are simply people who want the best for their people."

As they walked toward the famous Vatican vault, the pope grinned with a newfound respect for his unusually talented cloned friend. Once inside, Merlin and friends sat down with the pope, and Merlin quietly told him of his experience at the Vatican just before Urban's First Crusade. The pope hung on Merlin's every word as he recapped it all, including his knighted escorts to the Vatican and the magical extravaganza he'd happily provided. "Back then, it was like nothing anyone had ever seen before, and they treated me like a kind of royalty or demigod. It gave me a great sense of purpose to help people in need of relief from the wars and injustice that seeped into their lives every day. Through it all, I remained humble and blessed for everything God has granted me."

Chapter

21

The pope began to weep almost uncontrollably. Drying his eyes, he stood up, prompting Merlin to do the same, and he hugged his unusual friend again. After an impressive tour of the hi-tech underground vault, the pope was summoned back to his office for an unexpected, urgent call. His friend in the EU reported that his investigation, while still in progress, indicated that there were indeed a handful of Nazi superiors who had put out the order to contaminate the food, drug, and water supplies across Europe, using several key operatives. Their own spies within the party also reported that the contamination could eventually spread around the world, exactly as the pope's newest friends had warned. "We will extract the Nazi extremists with surgical precision, but unfortunately, the Freemasons are untouchable, my lord. My people believe that we may be too late already to prevent this event from taking place and that the time to act is now!"

The pope sighed deeply. "I am compelled to leave this most daunting task to you and your people. I will pray for your speedy success; please let me know when it is done, and God bless you and your men."

The pope caught up with his guests back at the library to break the good news. "They are now laying the groundwork to systematically remove the Nazi operatives and their commanders. He will let me know when it is done, and I will then in turn inform you. Until then, I will spend my time in silent prayer for forgiveness for us all."

Merlin went over to His Holiness and knelt. "My lord, believe me when I say that your ancient brother, the blessed Saint Urban, would be very proud of you right now."

The pope patted him on the shoulder and excused himself from the room. Looking at each other as though a great weight had just been lifted from their chests, the group suddenly noticed the intoxicating aroma of freshly cut roses from the garden. Joshua reminded them that there was still the matter of Gabriel and Seth to tend to. "They must be brought to justice and pay for what they've done and have conspired to do."

Frank then asked, "How do you suggest that we do that?"

With conviction Joshua added, "We stage a coup—all my English knightly brothers band together and expose them for the slimy parasites they truly are. It's time they knew."

Merlin said, "The minute the pope gives us the word that the Nazis are out of the equation, we head back to London and arrange a private meeting with your knights. We have a little time before we have to go, so for now, I suggest that we get ourselves well rested and prepare for our next move. I think I'll go back to the library to read for a while."

The others decided to take the grand tour and meet up for lunch later.

The next day, Merlin announced that it was time to go back to London to hold a secret meeting with Joshua's knightly brothers and get them up to speed and organized. "We have enough witnesses and evidence to put Gabriel and Seth behind bars and then some. Frank and I will inform our host of our intentions and meet you two back here with a taxi in one hour."

Fresh from the funeral and in his office, Gabriel tried his brand-new chair on for size and accessed his computer. He instantly noticed that someone had accessed his computer and saw Adolf's head turned toward the wall. He then quickly went to his closet and found that his prized golden dragon had been stolen. In a fit of rage, he summoned Seth, who was next door, relaxing with a violently bloody video game.

"Yes, my brother, Grand Master? What is your command?"

Gabriel moved closer to his number one, grabbed his lapels tightly, and pushed him up against the wall. "Someone gained access to my computer and probably downloaded copies of incriminating data and then stole my dragon. Now, I ask you—how is this possible? Do you realize what this means?" He slammed Seth against the wall again, almost rendering him unconscious. He then released him to allow him to catch his breath.

As he straightened his jacket, Seth said, "The intruders must be on video, my lord. I'll go down to the security room, see who they are, and take immediate action."

"We'll go together, Brother!" Gabriel said with an unusually wild glare Seth had not seen before.

They both entered the surveillance area, and Seth began to interrogate the chief night security guard. "Apart from the guests in the museum and library, the only visitors who entered the building in the past three days were the maintenance crew and the cleaning staff."

Seth promptly ordered the guard out, leaving Gabriel and himself alone to view the video feed. Finally, they saw the cleaning crew, who were in standard uniforms. Suddenly, Seth spotted a familiar face—Joshua's. He then saw Merlin's face glancing up at the camera and froze the image on the screen. With clinched fists and bulging eyes, Seth said, "Him! It can't be—I shot him dead at the hotel!" Seth moved closer to the screen, looking dumbfounded, as though he'd seen a ghost. "This is impossible—it can't be!"

About ready to explode, Gabriel responded, "He's either a copy of a clone, or you're a delusional moron; either way, it doesn't matter. What does matter is this." With a great deal of anxiety and little patience left, Gabriel snorted and snarled. "I have bled and sacrificed everything for this moment, and I'm not going to allow anyone to get in my way. They probably have enough evidence to put us away for life several times over. I want them found and killed—not tomorrow, but *today*—and, Seth, if you fail me again, one of us will be dead by morning—am I clear?"

With zero options available to him, Seth nervously replied, "After today, they will cease to exist, my lord; I swear it."

Seth left the hall and quickly ordered his unit to be assembled and ready to deploy in ten minutes.

Merlin and his friends touched down at Heathrow Airport that afternoon and took a taxi directly to their hotel. Once there, Joshua made the call to one of his knightly brothers, informing him of an emergency secret meeting in their hotel room in one hour. His brother instantly complied, and soon after, six plain-clothed, high-ranking Freemasons entered their hotel and stepped into Joshua's room. They were then instructed to sit quietly and listen to Joshua for the next thirty minutes.

"We always suspected Gabriel and Seth of having a different agenda, but this? Okay, lads, it would seem that it falls to us now, and we must act. Brother Dougherty, happens to be one of the top barristers in England and will begin working to build a strong case against brothers Gabriel and Seth immediately. Allow me to collect all the evidence with which to build an impenetrable case against them!"

The outspoken knight then made a couple urgent calls to some of his most trusted brothers from Interpol and Scotland Yard for support. Ten minutes later, he got off the phone. "My friends are on their way to detain Gabriel and Seth for questioning that will lead to their arrests within the hour. I recommend that we stay together for the time being until they're both apprehended."

Michelle casually glanced out the window and suddenly noticed a black Hummer and two black motorcycles parked in front of the hotel. With a sense of urgency on her face, she looked over at Merlin. He instantly looked concerned and got up to join her at the window, where they both saw Seth quickly exit the vehicle with two of his men. Merlin calmly but firmly whispered, "Gentlemen, I believe it's time for us to leave—right now!" He looked over to the knights. "You men take the stairs and go to Scotland Yard; we won't be far behind."

They all got up, wished their friends luck, and headed out toward the stairwell. Moving quickly, they scurried out to their vehicles and drove directly toward Scotland Yard.

Merlin, Joshua, Frank, and Michelle all went across the hall into Michelle's room and quietly waited by the door. Inside her room, looking through the peephole, Merlin watched as Seth and his men shot out the lock using silencers and entered the room. Then they heard the sound of a man, completely unhinged, screaming obscenities, like someone on the edge of insanity. After his childlike tantrum, Seth said, "They can't be very far; we'll keep to the shadows and wait for them around the perimeter of the hotel."

Upon leaving, appearing upset, Seth looked directly at the door that shielded Merlin and the others, and he moved toward the peephole, growling like a rabid dog. The madman finally vacated the room with his men, and afterward, Merlin and company entered to watch him get back into their vehicle and leave. Cautiously, Merlin and his group made their way down the stairs and safely into their vehicle and headed straight for the motorway. Seth's helicopter pilot then spotted a dark Mercedes leaving the hotel parking lot and informed Seth. Before doubling back on a wild-goose chase, Seth ordered his motorcycle units to catch up with the vehicle and report their findings.

The motorcycles were now close on either side of the Mercedes with darkly tinted windows, and the car's occupants began to stir with concern over being discovered. The man on the motorcycle closest to the driver's side firmly pointed to the shoulder of the road, prompting the Mercedes to pull over immediately. Merlin calmly said, "Please, I beg you all—just breathe deeply, and don't panic!" Instantly accessing the vehicle's mapping system to pinpoint Scotland Yard, he gunned the engine and swerved sharply, forcing one of the motorcycles into the river and the other into oncoming traffic.

The chopper pilot watched the occurrence and reported what had just happened directly to Seth. Then, with a certain level of renewed confidence, Seth said, "Our target, gentlemen, is the black Mercedes; lose them and you'll meet the same fate."

With moderate traffic in the heart of the city, Merlin took a detour to an empty side street, thinking they would be safe for the moment. The big black Hummer came out of nowhere, ramming one side of the Mercedes, visibly stunning the occupants inside.

Then, as quickly as it had appeared, the Hummer was gone. All at once, a police vehicle converged on the scene, and sighs of relief filled their car. Now at a complete stop, two police officers exited their car and slowly walked toward the damaged vehicle. Before anyone could say a word, both police officers silently collapsed to the ground, dead, in two pools of blood. The occupants all turned to see Seth in the passenger side of the Hummer, holding a pointed gun in their general direction.

He fired off four more shots into the car, shattering the windows and hitting Frank in the shoulder as Merlin sped off toward the motorway, with the Hummer in close pursuit. With the vehicles now side by side, Seth smiled at Merlin, showing him his gun and pointing it at Merlin's head. "I'm going to personally escort you to hell if I have to!"

Merlin used his telekinetic mind to close the Hummer's passenger window, trapping Seth's arm. He then forced the Hummer's steering wheel to veer to the left, moving them away from Merlin's car and into oncoming traffic. They just managed to miss two larger vehicles going the opposite direction and pulled over onto the shoulder to regroup and catch their breath. Seth turned to his driver and screamed, "Do that again, and I will end your days right here!" He pointed his gun at the driver's head. He then decided to order his trailer to the scene as the helicopter kept a close eye out.

In the backseat of the Mercedes, Joshua did what he could to stop the blood from flowing out of Frank's shoulder and to prevent Frank from losing consciousness. The Hummer was now back on track in high-speed pursuit, and it began to gain on Merlin just as the trailer arrived and got into position in front of the Mercedes. Seth got directly behind Merlin's vehicle and ordered the semi driver to open the back ramp. With the ramp fully lowered, sparking along the road, Seth ordered the driver to slow down. As he did, the Hummer rammed the car, pushing it up and into the trailer, and the ramp was raised shut, leaving the new captives shaken and in the dark.

"Is anyone else hurt?" Merlin said as he put the car in park, turned off the engine, and turned on the interior lights to see Frank passed out in the backseat. "How is he, Joshua?"

"He's lost some blood, but the bullet went clean through, and I think I've managed to stop the bleeding for now."

Michelle turned to Merlin and whispered, "He'll die if we don't get him to a hospital soon."

Merlin noticed that the mapping system in the car was out and said, "Joshua, check your phone to see if you have a signal!"

"It's dead—sealed in this reinforced, soundproof container, we're completely cut off." Now out of answers, Merlin felt beaten. As he searched for words, he slowly dropped his head.

"I have failed you all. My ego blinded me to certain realities. Huh, some prophet—I never saw this coming." Shaking his head, he said, "It was all for nothing, and for that, I am eternally sorry."

Michelle moved closer to Merlin and held his hand tightly. "You have nothing to be sorry for." She looked deeply into his teary eyes. "It is possible to do everything right and still lose. Life is perfect, but people are not."

They spent what seemed like an hour in silence, mentally preparing for the end, when the trailer came to an abrupt stop and the thick steel ramp door lowered behind them. Half expecting the trailer to be riddled with bullets, Joshua's knightly brothers entered the trailer, pleasantly shocking the captives. "Is everyone all right?" one of them shouted as Michelle, Joshua, and Merlin all shielded their eyes from the instant sunlight.

Joshua replied, "We have an injured man here; we need an ambulance right now!"

As they exited the trailer, they saw Seth and one of his men being escorted into the back of a police van. Merlin said loudly and clearly, "That man killed an Oxford professor, the Masonic grand master, and two police officers—that we know of."

A paramedic team carried Frank into a waiting ambulance as his concerned friends looked on. Merlin gently caressed Michelle and softly said, "You stay with Frank, and I'll see you back at the hospital very soon." He then hugged Joshua. "Thank you for your help and for trusting in me, my friend. I'll call you later to let you know how Frank's doing. In the meantime, go with your brothers to Scotland Yard, and let's finish this!"

Joshua replied. "Okay, but what about Gabriel?"

One of the lead detectives then said, "I have dispatched several police units to the Masonic hall for his immediate apprehension as we speak."

The sounds of sirens buzzed all around the great hall, and the officers heard a single gunshot from inside. There in his office, with his head on his desk in a pool of blood from an apparent self-inflicted gunshot wound to his temple, sat the lifeless body of Gabriel.

Merlin walked back up the ramp into the dark trailer and came out with the Mercedes. He gave Seth a smile and a wink just before he drove away.

An hour later, Joshua learned of Gabriel's demise and relayed the news to Michelle and Merlin, who were both now at the hospital.

Early the next day, asleep in the emergency waiting room, Merlin and Michelle were awakened by a nurse. "Your friend was lucky; he almost didn't make it. If he had come here any later, we would be having a very different conversation. He is awake, but he is weak and needs rest, so please be brief."

Inside Frank's hospital room, a sedated Frank opened his eyes as Merlin touched his good shoulder. "It's over, my brother. Seth was captured by police, and Gabriel is dead."

Overwhelmed and speechless, Frank responded with a smile as tears of joy trickled down his face. Merlin and Michelle both joined him with a few teardrops of their own, adding smiles all round.

A few short weeks later, the *London News'* front-page headline read "Masonic/Nazi Conspiracy Trial Set to Begin Today." Merlin and his friends all stood outside the courthouse and watched four officers and two detectives escort a cowering Seth in handcuffs and leg irons into the building. They were soon followed by all the Masonic knights in full dress, with Madame Sylvia leading the charge. Key European Union officials and, of course, the star witnesses—Merlin and friends—also attended the trial. The trial lasted only a few days, ending with the jury deliberating for a record twelve minutes before coming back with an overwhelming unanimous verdict of guilty on all counts. The presiding judge happily sentenced Seth to two back-to-back life sentences in a high-security prison, with no chance of parole. That day, the city came alive as though England had just won their first World Cup; cheers, handshakes, and hugs were witnessed everywhere. Abiding by Merlin's wishes, Joshua and his brothers did all the talking to the press as he, Michelle, and Frank left quietly out the back door to a waiting taxi.

On a plane headed back to the Vatican as requested by the pope, the heroes toasted to their victory with complimentary champagne. Later that day, they met with His Eminence in his office.

"My people informed me of all the details, and on behalf of the free world, I wanted to thank you all personally." His took a close look at Frank's arm sling, gently cupped his cheek, and said, "You are to spend three days in silent prayer repenting for your sins, and after that, Father DeCarlo, you are to be promoted to the rank of cardinal—if you so wish it."

Frank slowly dropped to one knee with the pope's help and humbly accepted this unexpected and generous offer.

"Splendid, my son—splendid!" the pope replied with a smile, as a proud father would. He then asked, "What of Joshua—why is he not here?"

"He has been very busy with his Masonic brothers and will soon be unanimously voted into the office of grand master," Merlin replied.

His Holiness asked Michelle what he could offer her as a reward.

"I've only ever wanted to travel and see the world," she excitedly said, holding on to Merlin's hand.

"Then so you shall, my dear." He took the Vatican gold card from Frank, handed it to her, and said, "Take a year, and I hope to hear all about it upon your return."

She humbly accepted, knelt, and kissed his ring. The pope then looked at Merlin. "You are, without a doubt, the most fascinating and enigmatic fellow I have ever had the distinct pleasure of meeting. First, I want you to know that wherever you go, there will always be a place for you here. I want you to think of the Vatican as a second home, but there must be something closer to your heart that I can do for you on a more personal level."

Merlin thought for a second or two. "I would love it if you were to allow me to put on a magic show for the Vatican and the local children tomorrow night—it's all that comes to mind."

The pope smiled and shook his head in complete wonder. "Ah, but there is something else. Without exposing your true identity, my cardinals and I have done some extensive historical research into your mother's obscure origin. We found that she was indeed worthy of a sainthood, and I took the liberty of having her canonized as Saint Arden. She died selflessly in northern Scotland, serving God during a savage atrocity, but not before birthing a child through immaculate conception—you. Not to imply that you are the son of God, but without a doubt, you are a very special man, to be sure."

Merlin's eyes welled up with tears, and he dropped down to one knee and kissed the pope's ring, thanking him for the thoughtful gesture. "I am humbled, without the words to postulate a fitting response, my lord."

The pope grinned, waited for Merlin to stand, and gave Merlin a big hug. "That will do, my boy—that will do." The content pope smiled, adding, "I feel just like the Wizard of Oz." They all laughed, except for Merlin, who looked curiously at Michelle, inconspicuously mouthing, *Wizard of Oz?*

Michelle affectionately laughed, put her arm around Merlin, and whispered, "We'll rent the movie."

The following night, Merlin put on an extravaganza that everyone, especially the children, thoroughly enjoyed. The grand finale was an elaborate fireworks display in which he lifted off the stage and dramatically disappeared into thin air right in front of everyone.

The next morning, Michelle and Merlin said tearful good-byes to Frank and the pope, promising to return the same time next year. They arrived back at Heathrow Airport the next day and headed out to the parking lot, where Merlin led her toward a brand-new motorhome. "Frank wanted to give us something special to remember him by. I couldn't say no, and I was hoping that you would—"

Before Merlin could finish his sentence, she threw her arms around his neck and gave him a long, passionate kiss, clearly saying yes. She wrapped her legs around him as they both slowly lifted a few inches off the ground for a while. Then they pulled away in their new vehicle, which had a personalized license plate that read OFF2OZ.